BONE
MAKER

a novel by

D. F. BAILEY

COPYRIGHT NOTICE

ACKNOWLEDGEMENTS

I am extremely grateful to Yvette Brend, Lawrence Russell, Rick Gibbs, and my wife Audrey for reading the early versions of *Bone Maker*. Their insights, wisdom and advice were invaluable to me as I worked through several drafts of the novel. — DFB

For more information about D. F. Bailey and to subscribe to his free newsletter, "Digital Words," visit dfbailey.com.

A death in the wilderness.

A woman mourns alone.

A reporter works a single lead.

※

Inspired by true events.

BONE MAKER

CHAPTER ONE

A WHIFF OF blood in the air.

The bear rose on his back feet, turned his head upwind and flared his moist nostrils. He needed food — anything to slake the deep hunger that clawed through his empty belly. The forest, thick with fir and cedar trees, surrounded him. In the distance he could see a blur of rocks on the hillside. His ears filled with the sounds of the spring melt rushing down the creek beds and the heavy tree limbs pulling in the wind. He listened for the sound of more gunshots and car engines but they had passed now. Still, he felt a lingering danger. He set his forepaws on the ground and made his way up the slope to the gravel road. He paused and looked along the muddy track and then walked with purpose toward his prey. As he approached, he could make out the scent of several men and their machines. He hesitated and moved forward again — a force of nature.

Hungry, willful, unrelenting.

※

When Ethan Argyle first caught sight of the bear he assumed it was a boulder that had fallen from somewhere above the ridge onto the gravel road. The bear stood motionless, hunched

1

forward, about a fifty yards up the track from the Mercedes GLK. But since something was obviously amiss with the car — the driver's window wide open, despite the late morning drizzle — neither Ethan nor his son Ben focussed on the animal. Until it began to move.

"Look at that, Dad." Ben pointed toward the bear with his gloved hand. He dug through his pocket for his binoculars. "It's big enough, but it *can't* be a grizzly. Not here." He pressed the glasses to his eyes, then gasped at the size of the animal gnawing away at something on the roadside. "Have a look," he whispered and passed the binoculars to his father.

"It's not a grizzly." Ethan focused the lens with the nose screw. "It's a black bear. He's feeding on something," he added but he couldn't make out what it might be. "No wonder we haven't come across any deer all day."

The father and son worked their way down the hill onto the switchback. There were dozens of dirt roads like this that cut through the forest above the coast, gravel tracks barely wide enough for two cars to squeeze past one another. But today no cars were visible and no trucks could be heard struggling up the long ravine. Nothing except the Mercedes, Ethan whispered to himself. The car looked abandoned; its engine was silent. A spray of mud caked the exterior, a dusty-gray paste that had hardened in the sun and then smudged under the light rain. He figured it had been parked here at least a day, since Saturday, when it had been sunny through the entire afternoon.

"There's just something wrong about that open window," Ben said as they approached the vehicle from the rear and then stopped about five feet away. He eased his rifle into the crook of his elbow and studied the car.

"Yeah." Ethan kept an eye on the bear, who seemed oblivious to them as it nuzzled a carcass on the roadside. They stood downwind from the animal and as Ethan sniffed the air he caught a whiff of fresh kill. "He can't smell us," he whispered to his son, "but he might hear us. Keep 'er quiet." He made a downward motion with his left hand and then brought his rifle from his shoulder into his arm. "Let's look at that window."

They walked silently beside the big SUV and peered into the black interior. It took a moment for his eyes to adjust to the lack of light, and only a few seconds longer for Ethan to make out the pool of blood that soaked the driver's seat. "Good lord!" he moaned, much louder than he wanted. He looked toward the bear to see if he'd startled.

"Jeez, I think that bear took him." Ben's voice was breathless. He wiped a hand over his mouth and angled the barrel of his gun towards the bear. A defensive move, nothing more. He kept his eyes on the bear, sure that it was more important than whatever might remain in the Mercedes.

"Doesn't make any sense," Ethan said and drew a long breath before he forced his head back through the top of the window. He could see the key fob lying in the CD tray. An opened pack of cigarettes, Marlboros, lay above the dash. A half-empty bottle of water stood uncapped in the drink caddy and beyond it a discarded Starbucks cup had spilled across the passenger seat. A rain jacket had been tossed onto the back seat and a duffle bag tucked in the rear footwell. He tried to imagine what could have transpired: a lone driver crossing the switchbacks is confronted by a rogue bear who refuses to yield an inch of the road ahead.

"He's starting to move, Dad. He might be onto us."

Ethan turned his attention to the scene up the road. The bear now stood upright over his kill with his eyes fixed on Ethan and Ben. Must be six hundred pounds, Ethan murmured to himself. The bear stole a step toward them and paused as if to consider his next move.

"I might have to take him out, Ben." His voiced sounded apologetic but firm.

"Yes sir." Ben stood behind his father and readied his gun. They'd done this a dozen times before when they were after deer. They hunted the old-fashioned way, with bolt-action Winchester 70 rifles. If one missed his shot, the second fired the insurance round. But Ben never had to make a shot like this. Not with his fingers this damp, his heart pounding.

The bear lurched another step forward, then charged. Ethan had to shoot before he was fully prepared. Still, when he fired, he thought he'd hit squarely in the bear's torso. The bear bobbed and weaved, paused to sneer with a look of puzzlement and then staggered forward again. A second later Ben fired his rifle. The bear roared and wheeled away as its front paw dissolved into a red pulp. It clambered into the scrub brush at the edge of the road, moaning loud wails that filled the depth of the ravine below.

"Damn. Now we have to go after it," Ethan murmured and fixed his jaw with a weary determination. "It's my fault, son," he said to dispel any misgivings the boy might have. He set their pace toward the bloody, abandoned carcass sprawled next to the weed-infested shrubs beside the road.

As they neared the corpse they staggered backward in an uneven motion that forced Ben to miss a step and move behind his father. The cadaver lay on its back, the chest cavity ripped open. Nothing of the man's throat — or his face — remained. Already the corpse was abuzz with flies.

"Oh no," Ben whimpered. He sunk to his knees and began to vomit onto the gravel.

"Give me your phone," Ethan said as he turned away from the mess that lay at their feet. "We've got to call the sheriff." As he punched 911 into the keypad, he prayed for a miracle. But he knew they were off the cellphone grid and they had little hope of connecting with anyone. They'd have to hike over to the switchback above the Lewis and Clark River where he'd parked the four-by-four, then drive down toward Astoria before they could make a cellphone connection.

He pulled his son by the forearm and braced him against his side. "Come on, it won't take us more than an hour," he said with forced certainty as he directed them back toward the ridge under Saddle Mountain.

Above them he saw two hawks surfing the aerial drafts in wide, easy circles. Somewhere below he could hear the bear crash through the bush, dashing loose rocks down the ravine into the rushing creek. Jesus, he moaned to himself and set his jaw once more. What kind of mess have we stumbled into this time?

CHAPTER TWO

"WELL, WELL, WELL. Will Finch — welcome back!" Wally Gimbel's wide face emerged from his office doorway when he saw Finch walk toward his cubicle at the far end of the writers' pool. Gimbel held his landline phone in one hand, the mouthpiece covered with a thumb.

"Good to see you," Will replied with a nod. Gimbel's face looked puffy and more inflamed than Finch remembered, but the voice retained the same edge of authority.

"Take a minute to dust off your keyboard," Wally whispered with a hint of fondness, an affection that he hoped the other reporters would not hear. "Then get back here in ten minutes." He winked and for a moment Finch imagined Wally was glad to see him again. "And bring Fiona Page with you," he added and turned his attention back to his phone call.

Finch continued down the aisle through the narrow labyrinth of walled pods known as "the bog" by the staff writers who complained that despite their urbane surroundings, they worked in a swamp seething with leeches and snakes. Most of them ticked away solemnly at their keyboards, a few others spoke in low tones to the digital images on their screens.

The reporters had quickly learned the optimal volume to employ during Skype calls: a narrow spectrum between barely audible, and a murmur which could not be heard in the adjacent pods.

No one made eye contact with Finch until he reached Fiona Page's station. "Will!" Surprised, she pulled the earbuds from under her hair and leaned back in her chair. "Welcome back," she said and wheeled her chair to one side and waved Finch toward the guest chair.

"Thanks." He forced a smile and dropped onto the padded seat. Settled below the five-foot wall baffle, he was now invisible to everyone else in the bog. Hiding in the trenches, he thought. A good place to spend his first few minutes back on the front line.

"I didn't realize you were coming back this week." She pulled a length of hair over her shoulder and tipped her head to one side. "Sorry to hear the news." She frowned and looked away. Then she smiled a genuine good-to-see-you grin that flecked the dimples in her cheeks.

"Back at it," he said halting a little, unsure how much she knew about his situation. About Bethany and Buddy. And everything that happened after that. He forced himself to focus on the job. "So did you pick up the threads on the Whitelaw trial?"

"You bet." She opened a file on her screen and tilted it in case he wanted to have a look at her notes. "Not much to report over the last month, but I can send this to you if you want." Her tone was back-to-business.

He was silently thankful to her for immediately forcing him

back into the game. Into the chase where they hunted and pecked out their daily nourishment from the world of politics, fame, sex, money, and crime — and the attempt to make sense of it all.

"Sure. Forward it, but only if Wally wants me back on the story." Finch nodded toward the managing editor's office. "By the way, he wants to see us both in five minutes in the board-room."

The boardroom doubled as the staff meeting room at the *SF eXpress*, the internet division of the *San Francisco Post*. Willie Parson, the *Post's* CEO (and with his brother, co-owner of Parson Media) explained that the "e" denoted "electronic" and the "X" meant there would be no press machines cranking out actual papers. And no more press union, machine operators, typesetters, bundlers, truckers or paper carriers.

Like everyone else at the *eXpress*, Finch had quickly accepted Wally Gimbel's invitation to help him establish the digital version of the *Post*. If Finch had rejected Wally's offer he would have enjoyed a direct exit onto the street with a week's pay for every year of service in the old newsroom. Six years in his case. Three for Fiona. Dozens of reporters, many with more seniority, weren't offered any opportunities within the paper — print or internet. And when the cuts hit they came fast and hard. No good-bye parties, no chance to see the old news hounds off to another, better life. As far as management was concerned, the shame of teetering bankruptcy outweighed any loyalty to dismissed veterans.

"He'll want you back on the story," she said with certainty. "Did you hear what happened this weekend?"

He nodded no.

Before she could fill him in, her phone buzzed. She picked up her handset, listened a moment and said, "Okay, Wally."

"That was less than ten minutes," Finch grumbled as he followed her toward the boardroom. He hadn't even seen his old pod, let alone dusted off the keyboard.

※

From the look in Gimbel's eyes, Finch figured a new crisis had hit. Something lower on the Richter scale than presidential assassination or global financial collapse, more likely another horrible mass shooting, or perhaps the long-anticipated closure of the newspaper.

"What's up?" he asked and leaned against the doorframe as Gimbel eased into a swivel chair at the head of the massive oak table. If needed, the boardroom could accommodate the entire digital-edition staff, stringers and freelancers. Roughly twenty people, ten sitting around the table (snatched by Gimbel from his old editorial office downstairs), with latecomers allotted to standing room only. Fiona stood beside Finch and then sat next to her boss.

"Close the door." Gimbel rolled his lower lip under his teeth and tapped a finger on his tablet screen. "You read the news feed this morning?"

Fiona shrugged with a sense of resignation. "Yeah ... it's hard to believe."

Finch raised his hands. "No time, Wally. Haven't even set eyes on my desk yet." He shrugged, a plea for a time out, and then realized he wasn't part of the game. *I need to suit up and join the team,* he told himself and walked behind Gimbel and sat on his left. They hunched together in the windowless room and stared at the list of links on the tablet screen.

Gimbel looked into Finch's eyes. He wanted to test the reaction, witness the surprise voltage on his face. "Ray Toeplitz is dead."

"Ray Toeplitz?" Finch glanced away. "Dead?"

Gimbel tapped his finger on the computer screen. A window popped open revealing the headline: *Key Witness Dies Tragically.* Below the text stood a picture of Toeplitz's worried face as he exited the front doors of the Hall of Justice two months earlier.

"It gets weirder than you think," Fiona said and let this idea sink in before continuing. "Did you hear that crazy story on Sunday? About a black bear dragging some guy from his Mercedes in the backwoods in Oregon — and eating him alive?" She paused to see if this registered, examined Finch with a hint of absolution, knowing that if he'd skipped the news over the past month it was understandable. Everyone understood.

In fact, Finch had purposely ignored all the news — TV, radio, papers, the web. He ignored her questions and set his eyes on Gimbel. "So what's the connection?"

Wally clicked on another link and the article about the rogue bear flashed onto the screen. "Toeplitz."

"What?" Finch brushed a hand over his mouth and quickly scanned the story. When he finished, he tipped back in his chair and gazed at the ceiling. Toeplitz: the genius with a PhD in Finance Mathematics. In his early twenties he'd made his mark on Wall Street, engineering complex hedge fund strate-

gies that funneled millions into traders' bank accounts. Ten years ago he'd been hired by Whitelaw, Whitelaw & Joss and then promoted to the position of Chief Financial Officer.

But was Toeplitz a player in the Mt. Gox bitcoin scam in Japan? Maybe. And was he part of the financial manipulations that defrauded investors of over four hundred and fifty million dollars? Possibly. Although he vehemently protested his innocence, as a member of his company's Board of Directors, Toeplitz was arrested and accused of fraud in a trial which everyone assumed would last at least six months. The tabloids called it "The Battle for Bitcoin."

But recently Toeplitz experienced a moral epiphany, or more likely, Finch assumed, he'd negotiated a compelling plea bargain with the District Attorney. Whatever his motivation, Toeplitz said he possessed records pointing to a massive fraud perpetrated by the senator's step-brother, Dean Whitelaw. And so Toeplitz decided to take the stand as a prosecution witness against Senator Franklin Whitelaw's investment house.

The senator himself claimed prosecutorial immunity because all his business affairs were held in a blind-trust, which he referred to as a "Chinese Wall." Another racist gaff from the politician who'd built a populist reputation on similar foot-in-mouth blunders. Republicans loved him. Democrats laughed. Five times he'd been elected and sent to Washington.

And now came this latest episode in the most bizarre corporate saga that Finch had ever covered. Somewhere in a remote coastal forest, Raymond Toeplitz had been devoured by a bear.

Finch turned his attention back to Wally. "So there is a natural justice, after all."

"Mmm." Wally pressed his lips together and shrugged doubtfully. "I hope not, especially if we can squeeze new juice from this story. With the executive team in Parson Media threatening to roll the print edition of the *Post* back to three days a week, it would be helpful if your tale of Toeplitz and the bear could draw in a few more readers. Just to keep their office doors open another week or two." He pointed toward the floor, to the offices one story below.

They all smiled at this, at the fantasy that the digital division might save the print edition from insolvency. In any case, Finch felt relieved to have the story pitched in his direction. Something substantial to chew on instead of the bitter fruit of Bethany's guilt and depression. And the tragedy with Buddy.

"All right." Finch sat up in his chair. A jolt of energy radiated through his chest. In his gut he could feel the story coming back to life. He never expected the fraud trial to reach a satisfying conclusion. Now a new chapter opened before them. Everything had changed. "So. Fly to where? Portland? Interview the local sheriff, the coroner, and whoever bagged the bear. Right?"

"No." Gimbel smiled with a miser's grimace. "*Drive* to Astoria, the county seat of Clatsop County. Check the map. It's on the rear end of the back of beyond. Take the company car," he added after he remembered the photo of Finch's destroyed Toyota. A total write-off. "And so far, no one has found the bear, dead or alive. But don't let that stop you. Everyone loves to talk about the one that got away. I'm sure if anyone can pick up the story from there, you can." He turned to Fiona. "Meanwhile, I want you to develop the human angle. For the first time, Toeplitz appears as a victim in this sorry tale. Did he have a wife? Kids?"

"No." Finch shook his head. "No family at all. He was a childless orphan." An interesting combination, he thought and then realized it was a circumstance he and Toeplitz now shared: no parents, no siblings, no spouse, no children.

Gimbel paused. "Then get Dean and Franklin Whitelaw's reaction to Toeplitz's demise. If he stonewalls you try Senator Whitelaw's sons. They're twins. The two boys were brought into the firm in the last few years. They probably knew Toeplitz, too. Or his daughters, there's two or three of them. Remember, both of you, we don't work at a news*paper* anymore. We're looking for the human dimension here — opinions, rumors, innuendo — not *just* the facts." This was Gimbel's new mantra based on his theory that print delivered news while the internet delivered opinion. Overall, Finch had to agree.

"You got it." Fiona pulled her notes together and rose from her seat. "I'll email you the files I gathered over the last month," she said to Finch and pursed her lips, a sign that read: buckle up, we're both in for a long ride.

Finch stood, ready to follow her when Wally raised a hand and said, "Hold up a minute, Will. I've got a few questions for you."

※

Wally seemed nervous. A rare moment of hesitation gripped him. "I didn't have time to check in with you." His head wavered from side to side. "I mean about what kind of workload you can handle right now. Do you think you're ready for this?"

Finch shrugged. Good of you to ask, he thought, but what I need more than anything is to slide into the old groove. More than that, to get back into my life. "I'm ready. Hell, I'm here a week earlier than anyone expected," he said with a curt nod, and when he realized Gimbel needed more assurance he added, "Look, this new angle on Toeplitz might ease me back into the routine. After a day's drive through the Redwoods, maybe I can step into the Whitelaw story through the back door."

"Good." Gimbel raised his eyes from the oak table and studied Finch's face, unsure if he could carry the load so soon. "You know, normally we wouldn't send anyone up to Oregon to dig through this mess with Toeplitz. A few phone calls would reel in the details. But since you're back a week early and still technically on medical leave, it might prove a good way to bring you in." Gimbel raised his eyebrows as if to add, so don't treat it as a vacation.

When Finch sensed that his reliability was the issue he leaned forward and stared into his editor's eyes. "Wally, look … it's over. It's been thirty-three days." To lighten the mood he faked a smile, checked his watch and said, "Make that thirty-four."

Gimbel gazed at Finch with an expression that softened his face. Not with pity, but with an air of empathy.

Finch could understand his concern. Gimbel had assembled the *eXpress* team only ten months ago. And eight months in, just as the Whitelaw trial began to gather a national following, Finch's calamity hit. Wally had to assign Fiona to cover the trial while Finch checked out of the bog and into Eden Veil Center for Recovery. The bucolic retreat provided the space

Will needed to come to terms with the black pit into which he'd stumbled, and then been shattered.

"I'm okay now. The time off did me some good. Really. It's over, I've picked myself up and I know I have to move on," he said and swept his hand toward the wall. "It's all about my job now. That's what I do." The palm of his hand hit the table. "*This* is who I am now."

Gimbel tipped his head to one side. "All right," he whispered and set his fist against his mouth. He shifted his weight, a signal the meeting might soon be over, but then he settled again and angled his wide face toward his reporter. "And what about Bethany?"

Finch leaned back in his chair, a bit startled. This was getting personal. Six months ago, once they could trust one another, Wally had mentioned Bethany's drinking. Said he knew where it could lead, that he'd lived through something similar himself. Will realized that his boss needed some assurance that this part of Finch's world wouldn't blow up again. "I haven't seen her in thirty-five days. She's...." He looked into his open hands, at the emptiness they held. "Look … she's completely broken." He narrowed his eyes. "You want the honest truth?"

Gimbel nodded.

"With luck, I'll never see her again."

Gimbel pressed his lips together and drew a long breath. "I know you think this is none of my business, but I need to know if you can stick this thing."

Stick this thing? What did that mean? Could Finch stick with the job — or stick a knife into the part of his life destroyed by Bethany and surgically remove the diseased tissue? He fixed his eyes on the far wall. "Okay. Here's the bare essentials, for your ears only: she's been suspended from her job, with pay, pending the medical examiner's report and criminal investigation. Likely there'll be a trial for criminal negligence, maybe manslaughter. I hope so. If that sounds like revenge, then so be it. I'll take my slice served cold." His eyes narrowed. "As for me, I've moved into a one-bedroom place on South Van Ness while I'm looking for something better." He felt as though he'd just climbed a steep flight of stairs. If nothing else, at least he still held a grip on the facts of his life.

Will had a sense that his managing editor wanted more, that he wanted to hear something about Buddy. But he felt that if either of them uttered Buddy's name, some kind of emotional disaster could follow.

"South Van Ness?" Wally Gimbel shook his head doubtfully, then smiled, happy to divert their attention.

"Do you know how hard it is to find a place in San Francisco for two thousand dollars?" Will tried to fix a grin on his lips but instead looked away.

"All right," Wally said and exhaled another long breath, a sigh of relief that they'd both survived this conversation — a topic that they had to resolve before they could move forward. "I'm going to give you a week," he concluded. "Then you tell me if you can stick it."

CHAPTER THREE

DONNEL SMEARDON EASED the pack from his shoulders and checked to ensure his sweater and lunch bag covered the baggie of weed that Ben Argyle had ordered. Or demanded, was more like it. Then he jumped on his bike and coasted down the slope toward Astoria High School. He made a point of stopping at each intersection. Better to be safe than get busted again by another over-zealous cop. *Talk about too much time on their hands.* Especially now that Washington and Colorado had legalized pot. Rumor had it that Oregon might be next. He wondered if the new laws would put him out of business. Maybe. Or maybe he'd just have to move his product line up-scale. Crack, coke, H? The big leagues. He leaned forward and squeezed the hand brakes. Something about dealing heroin made him nervous.

"Donnel!"

He brought the bike to a stop and looked into the alley off Jerome Avenue. Ben Argyle stood next to a cedar board fence, a worried look drawn across his face. Ben was pissed, Donnel was sure of that. And he'd feel even worse once Donnel delivered the bad news.

D. F. Bailey

"Hey, Ben." He hopped off his bike and parked it against the fence, then looked down the length of the gravel lane to see if anyone could sneak up on them. Coast clear, he slipped the pack onto the crossbar of his bike and began to unzip the inner pocket. "I got it."

"You better," Ben said but when he considered the look on Donnel's face he added, "Got *what?*"

"The greens, man. Jesus, what else?"

"Greens? What are you talking about?" Ben scanned the alley and tried to focus on what he needed to say. "Look, my dad is going to shit if you don't give his pistol back to me."

Donnel Smeardon had his hand on the baggie of marijuana. He decided to wait a moment, to let things drift. Then he pressed forward. "You want this pot, or not?"

"Not now." Ben curled his hands into fists and walked in a tight circle. "Fuck the pot."

"Fuck the pot?" He zipped the pouch shut and stared at Ben. "Yesterday it was *give* me the pot. You were like Robert Fucking DeNiro for some greens. Now it's *fuck* the pot?"

Ben squeezed his fists and for a moment tried to consider the options. The more he thought about their situation, the more he realized he had none. Soon he'd have to confess everything.

"Look, Dad inspects his guns every month. It's like an obsession with him. If I don't get that Glock back by Friday I know he's going to the cops to report it. He has to. Don't you *get* that? As far as he's concerned it's a stolen weapon." He paused to see if this made any sense to Donnel. When he saw the dazed look in Donnel's eyes he realized he needed *some-*

18

thing to make this better. Why had he ever agreed to help Donnel Smeardon? Another mystery. Unanswerable.

"Look, the cops are going to talk to everyone. Including me. Including *you,* Donnel." He nodded his head with a sense of dread. "You said you needed it for *one* night. That was two weekends ago. Shit, why don't you just give it back to me?"

Donnel pulled the pack straps over his shoulder and straddled his bike. "There's problems, man."

Ben leaned forward and pulled the left strap on Donnel's pack into his hand. "Look, you've got to give me something. And right now."

"Fuck you." Donnel couldn't miss the terror in Ben's eyes. The depth of his fear unnerved him. "All right, just chill, okay?"

"Chill? You don't get it. I want that gun. And *right* now." He clenched his fist.

"All right, man. Here." Donnel dug into the patch pocket on his jeans and presented an iPhone to Ben. "It's an iPhone 6, man. Totally jail-breaked." He passed the phone to Ben and tipped his head. "Probably costs more than your fucking Glock."

Ben took the phone, gazed at it briefly and shoved it into his pocket. "You'll get this back when I get the pistol," he said. "And that better be by Friday."

"Like I said, there's problems. Stuff you don't want to know about."

"I don't want to know?" Ben could feel his chest tighten. "You don't want to know what's going to happen if Dad calls you on this."

"You mean if he calls *you*, on it." Donnel pushed off with both feet and yelled over his shoulder. "Don't worry, you'll have it by Friday afternoon. Saturday morning at the latest."

Ben watched Donnel glide toward the school and wondered how he'd get through the rest of the week knowing the creep was likely to screw up so bad they'd both go down for this. His worst fear concerned the crushing disrespect from his father and mother. And there could be legal problems. Depending on what Donnel had done with the gun. Serious charges, even a trial. He bunched his fists together and could feel tears welling in his eyes. The fact that his father was a teacher at his school only made things worse. He brushed the tears away with his jacket sleeve and trudged forward, for the first time in his life feeling the burden of a condemned soul.

※

On Tuesday evening Finch arrived in Astoria and checked into the Prest Motel. He decided to begin unravelling the story of Toeplitz's death from the most authoritative source possible — the county sheriff. On Wednesday morning he drove up 7th Street to the gray, two-story Victorian building and parked the company car, a Ford Tempo, at the curb. Minutes later the receptionist pointed to the sheriff and said he was just about to take a break.

"Coffee's on me," Finch told him when they shook hands. At first the sheriff tried to put Finch off, but when the reporter explained that he only needed a few quotes and some color commentary about the bear attack, Sheriff Gruman waved a hand and told Finch to follow his squad car down to Three Cups Coffee House.

"No worries. Coffee's always on the house for me," he said. "But you can pay your own."

Once he settled into the restaurant booth and set his notepad and phone recorder on the table, Finch looked at Sheriff Mark Gruman and studied his gnarled face. Gruman rubbed the scrub of whiskers on his goatee, rolled his eyes and looked away. His grizzled look matched the weariness of his manner, his pock-marked cheeks, the scars of adolescent acne. Finch imagined that he'd suffered from it as a kid. Social stigma, shunning — the sort of marginalization any fifteen-year-old might endure due to his appearance.

"You might not know this," Gruman said, "but my staff have been cut by over half. During emergencies I have to deputize the locals. We call them *swear-ins*. Stick around long enough and you'll be one of 'em." He leveled his torpid gaze at the reporter to confirm this was no joke. "I'm so flat out busy, I don't even know if I've got *time* to talk to the press." He pronounced press as though it began with a capital P, suggesting a rare brush with celebrity.

"Same story in my world, sheriff." Guessing that it was a little early in the conversation to address him by his first name, Finch leaned closer as if he were sharing a mutual secret. "The newspaper industry is in tatters. I had to move over to the internet side of things to hang onto my job."

Gruman dismissed this with a curt frown and gazed through the window.

The restaurant faced the remarkably wide mouth of the Columbia River. At this time of day the Three Cups Coffee House sat in the shadow of the exit ramp off the Astoria-

Megler Bridge. The view, expansive and clear, captivated Finch.

"I had no idea the river was so broad."

"When the fog sets in, you can't see the far side," Gruman said. "It's fourteen miles to get over to Washington."

"Fog's like that in San Francisco, too." Finch lifted a glazed fritter in his right hand, smiled and nudged the side plate of desserts that he'd ordered toward the sheriff.

Gruman took a bite from a chocolate donut and set it aside. "Frisco." He nodded with a sense of distant familiarity as he chewed on his donut. "We used to go almost every summer when I was a kid. Stayed with an uncle and aunt in Oakland. Frankly, it put me off cities generally," he added with a wince.

"I can see why you live here." Finch cast his eyes out to a rusty-looking freighter sliding under the bridge toward Asia. "Beautiful place. No question."

The conversation was headed nowhere. Years of personal interviewing had taught Finch that empathy is the key to unlocking the most reticent personality. This primary principle was most effective whenever he had to deal with legal professionals, the people who knew the law by rote and could easily shield themselves from the duel of interrogation. *"I don't have to talk to you."* This sentence — or its many variations — was a typical defensive parry. Whenever Finch heard a lawyer, cop, judge, or detective utter these words he'd pause and then with a renewed sense of sympathy he'd say, "Look, I'm on your side. To ensure your point of view gets heard."

But Gruman wasn't about to open any doors. If he had something personal to hide, Finch wouldn't know it. He tried to steer Gruman back to Toeplitz's misadventure with the black bear. He'd already explained that since he'd covered most of the Whitelaw trial, the story of Toeplitz's demise was the necessary bookend to the entire narrative.

"With the little time I do have I'll tell you one thing," Gruman said wiping his lips with a paper napkin. "One thing totally out of the ordinary."

Finch leaned closer and his eyebrows knit together.

"The window on the driver's side of the Mercedes was rolled all the way down." Gruman's eyes widened and he smiled as if he still couldn't believe it. "There was no breakage of any kind. Obviously that bear, if we could find him, could tell us a lot. But one thing is sure: he didn't have to break that window to haul Toeplitz from his car." He devoured the last morsel of his donut, sucked his fingertips, then wiped them with the napkin while he considered Toeplitz's situation. "Which has to make you wonder. Did Toeplitz stop the car before the bear appeared? Open his window for a breath of air? Did he have some kind of heart attack?" Gruman put these questions to Finch, certain that their answers could provide the only explanation for Toeplitz's death.

"The autopsy might show that," Finch said and made a note on his coil pad.

"Autopsy? Believe me, when I drove up there I could tell in two seconds that there was very little to examine, apart from a few scattered extremities." Gruman sneered and tipped his head to suggest that Finch didn't have a clue about the extreme trauma of Toeplitz's final moments. "If you want to, check with Jennie Lee, the county medical examiner."

"Jennie Lee." He scrawled another note. "What about the crime scene report?"

Another dismissive sneer, this time broad enough to suggest that Gruman was tiring of Finch's questions. "What *crime?* I guess to some of your readers, this all might seem like an offense against nature. Or by nature. But really, Mr. Finch, isn't this story just a notch or two above dog-bites-man?" He sipped his coffee and stalled to see the response to this piece of logic. But Finch waited until he continued. "I suppose the headline to your story might be 'Murder by Nature.'" Gruman smiled a snaggletoothed grin. He seemed quite pleased with this flash of inspiration.

Finch pressed his lips together and looked away. He despised cops who tried to instruct him in the niceties of his own job. But he needed to keep Gruman on his side. He decided to change tack. "What about the Mercedes?"

"Bob Wriggly towed it into town. He's storing it up in his lot. Nice set of wheels. It's now part of Toeplitz's estate. I expect the probate lawyers will keep it off limits."

Maybe, Finch thought. But likely that was a pretty low priority right now. He made a note of Wriggly's name and continued. "And the hunters who found him?'

Gruman finished his coffee and lifted his hat in his left hand. "Ethan and Ben Argyle. School teacher and his boy. Most weekends they're somewhere up in the hills. Preppers — like a dozen other people around here. They all stockpile brown rice and beans in their root cellars. They're friendly enough, though. You can reach Ethan at Astoria High School. He might take you up there." He eased his legs from under the table and stood.

Again, Finch noted their names and then got to his feet and shook the sheriff's hand. Gruman stood at least four inches taller than the reporter. "You mind if I tell Ethan Argyle we were talking?"

This question forced Gruman to pause. A look of hesitation — or regret that he'd revealed too much — passed over his face. Then he leaned forward to look at Finch directly. "Course not. And ask him to say 'hello' to Millie for me."

"Thanks, Mark." Finch smiled, happy to dangle his first name before him. A breach of the sheriff's self-esteem, or protocol perhaps, but it allowed Finch to push open a door that had separated them. "One last question. Do we know why Toeplitz was driving up those switchback logging roads the day he died?"

Gruman ran his tongue along the edge of his upper teeth. He shrugged. "Maybe I'll read about that when you find out, Will. On your blog, next time I log onto your internet newspaper."

Finch walked Gruman to the door, then raised a hand in the air as if he'd forgotten something. "Pit stop," he said and waved toward the bathroom. "Good talking to you."

Gruman frowned once more, his standard expression Finch realized, and as he turned toward his car the sheriff called out, "Any time."

※

Finch walked back to the cashier and asked her for directions to Bob Wriggly's towing operation, the medical examiner's office, and Astoria High School. Because the Mercedes would soon be cleaned up and moved off his premises by the estate lawyers, he knew he had to find Wriggly immediately. But first he called the high school and made an appointment to see Ethan Argyle and his son when school let out. A second call landed him an early-afternoon meeting with Jennie Lee.

Twenty minutes later he pulled into Wriggly's property off Navy Pipeline Road. A dirt track rose through an open gate that led to a cedar-sided cabin on the left and an old barn that had been converted into a combination garage and auto-wrecking operation. At least fifty abandoned cars and trucks littered the gravel path up to the door where a man stood in grease-caked overalls, his fists bunched on his hips, staring down at Finch.

"Lost?" he called out.

"Not if you're Bob Wriggly," he said as he climbed out of his car. He smiled and held out a hand. "Will Finch. I was hoping to talk to you."

The mechanic waved his hand in the air, his knuckles and palm smudged with grease. "Good to meet you, but shaking my mitt won't help you any." He laughed, happy with this small joke.

Finch realized that Wriggly was the opposite of Gruman — warm, generous, eager to please. He explained that he was a reporter following the Whitelaw trial in San Francisco and trying to make some sense of Toeplitz's death.

"Don't know anything about Whitelaw. Or Toesplits. Or whatever his name is," he said as he adjusted a baseball cap over the gray hair that spiked past his ears. "But I know a few things about that Mercedes GLK."

"Nice car, huh?"

Wriggly tipped his head toward Finch's Ford Tempo and over to his own vehicle, an Econoline van sporting a dozen stickers for rod and gun clubs plastered over a series of festering rust patches. "Nicer than yours or mine." He laughed a little and then his voice flattened. "At least before that bear yanked him out of there. So what can I do to help?"

As easy as that, the door opened. Once a month Finch encountered the Bob Wrigglys of the world, people who live open, honest lives and no matter their age — Wriggly looked about sixty — they're never warped by cynicism or some other funk that grips so many people.

"Sheriff Gruman told me you towed Toeplitz's car out of the hills. If you've got it parked somewhere, I'd like to have a look. Take a picture or two," he said and lifted his cell phone in one hand, "just so I have an image for the article I promised my editor tonight."

Wriggly nodded toward the barn. "You email it in?"

Finch smiled. "Hopefully before midnight. Otherwise I catch hell."

"I bet," Wriggly said and he led the way toward the barn. He yanked the sliding door to the left, flipped a set of switches, and the garage reverberated with the sound of overhead fluorescent lamps sputtering to life.

An instant later the room was flooded with light. Finch was surprised by the tidy interior space. At the far end, an exterior door leading onto the forest stood ajar. One wall, racked with an array of tools, faced a full-service mechanical shop. A 1967 Mustang was aloft on a hoist and beside it, enclosed behind a chain-link fence, stood a black Mercedes GLK. The loose fencing around the car was secured with an Ace padlock. At a glance, Finch knew that any street kid could break it open in a few minutes.

"That's Toesplits's." Wriggly chuckled as if couldn't get over the name.

"Can you open the gate? Just for a few pics."

Wriggly considered this a moment, then walked to one of the tool chests, and pulled a key into his fist. He paused and set the key back in place. "You know, I'd best not. Sheriff insisted it wasn't part of a crime scene — the car wouldn't be allowed here if it was — but Jennie Lee ordered me to leave everything as is and secure the car behind the fence until she files her report."

Finch stepped up to the fence. "I heard the driver's window was wide open." His voice dropped to a whisper, but Wriggly could still hear him.

"Still is. I haven't touched a thing. Despite the smell."

"Lee's the county medical examiner?" He paced in front of the fence, scanning for irregularities.

"She is that." Wriggly nodded and watched him step away. "And more."

"And *more?*"

"Woman's on the move. I give her another few months to make her mark here, then move on to Portland. Can't blame her; she's an outsider."

Finch considered this. An outsider. Unlike Gruman and Wriggly. "And she told you there might be something more to this?"

"No." Wriggly shrugged and Finch glanced at him, a look

to encourage him to go on. "Nothing more to it, it's just ... incomplete."

"Incomplete?" Finch studied him a moment, waiting for him to elaborate. When he offered nothing more than a frown, Finch turned the conversation to the bear. "Have you ever seen this kind of thing before?"

"Never. But I've read about it." Wriggly shrugged. "Every few years somewhere in the northwest you hear stories about rogue bears."

"Yeah, I've read them, too," Finch said and slid the phone back into his pocket. Before he left San Francisco, he'd googled black bear attacks. They were rare, but often severe and sometimes deadly.

After a few minutes, as Wriggly walked the reporter back to the Ford Tempo, he cleared his throat and spat on the gravel. "Don't you think it's a little odd that Toesplits's car is being stored here?"

Finch pondered the deeper question drawn in Wriggly's face. "Why? After an accident don't you store cars like this while the lawyers probate the estate?" He smiled, thinking they were in this together now, and in all of Oregon, Bob Wriggly was the best friend he had.

"Never. It's either secured by the sheriff in the police compound for analysis or evidence. But if the tow job is considered a private fare, I'm left to deal with it as I see fit," he said. "I've never been told by the medical examiner to keep a car under lock and key. Never been told to leave blood smeared all over the seats. Not like that," he said and crooked a thumb back toward the garage. "This is different."

Will considered the problem. "So Gruman wanted the car *out* of police custody, but Janice Lee wanted to keep it under surveillance. I guess that runs a little contrary to my experience with cops. But I've only just met Gruman. Seems like he's overworked. Maybe he doesn't want the trouble."

"Maybe not." Wriggly turned his head doubtfully.

Finch glanced around Wriggly's yard and tried to judge the quickest way to drive to the medical examiner's office. On the left past Wriggly's gate he could see the dirt track cut up the hill toward a thick stand of cedar trees. "If I go up the hill can I find my way back into town?"

"Eventually. But the only house up there is Mark Gruman's place."

"The sheriff?"

"Craziest collection of wood-n-nails this side of Portland. A Geodesic dome hand-built by our local hero. Looks like it, too."

Finch turned his head. "Local hero ... what does that mean?"

Wriggly nodded with a grudging respect. "Won himself a bronze star in Iraq. That's why he's always elected county sheriff. Four terms running. Maybe five." He lifted his ball cap, scratched the rag of silver hair with his free hand. "Yeah, he was in Desert Storm. Got himself a reputation over there. The boys called him the Bone Maker."

CHAPTER FOUR

LESS THAN AN hour later Will Finch was trying to keep pace with Jennie Lee. The county medical examiner was a lean, thirty-year-old physician and forensic pathologist — and a paragon of fitness and health. The opposite of the daylight-phobic stereotype portrayed in most CSI dramas, Jennie marched along a hillside trail above Astoria with a vigor that glowed in her face.

"Despite what you might think, normally this case wouldn't rate a forensic autopsy," Jennie pronounced without a gasp. "In these cases — death by misadventure — our mandate is simply to determine the cause of death, confirm the identity of the corpse and then restore the remains to a state of dignity. Which, in the Toeplitz case, was impossible."

"That bad, was it?" Finch hauled in a lungful of air and inwardly rejoiced to see Jennie pull over at a cliffside view-point. From time to time he caught a glimpse of the wide mouth of the Columbia River and the green hills of Washing-ton State in the distance. Perhaps she'd pause here for five or ten minutes.

Jennie ignored the question and studied the view. "Now

there's a sight most Americans would give their eye teeth to savor once in a lifetime. Me, I get to see it every day. I'm glad you caught me when you did. Just in time for my daily constitutional."

Constitutional. Finch pondered the possibilities. A few superficial clues suggested that she was a fairly traditional woman, perhaps even a Republican.

"The best way to enjoy the highlights. Follow the locals, right?"

"When in Rome," he mused and stood a moment in silence as the panic in his lungs subsided. He realized that Jennie had an obligation to maintain the confidentiality of Toeplitz's autopsy, but he hoped that if he kept his requests to verifying the facts, Jennie might begin to trust him. "My editor told me that the car registration and his license identified the vehicle owner as Ray Toeplitz. That seems clear. But did the DNA from the corpse confirm his identity?"

Jennie shifted her eyes from the river to Finch. "You mean was I able to determine if the corpse found on the side of the road was that of the car's registered owner?"

"Yes." He glanced away. This could take a while, he realized. She was much more litigious than most MEs that he'd met. Perhaps the most by-the-book person he'd ever encountered. He forced a smile to his lips. "Exactly. In other words, was the body that of Raymond Toeplitz?"

Jennie shifted her feet, half-turning to face him. "Did you know Mr. Toeplitz?"

Finch nodded and realized he had to offer her something. "Not well, but I've interviewed him. Twice, in fact."

"Twice?" Jennie cocked her head and crossed her arms.

"Once when his employer, Whitelaw, Whitelaw & Joss, was exposed in a massive fraud. A little less than year ago now."

Jennie blinked and raised a hand to her chin. "I remember that. Something to do with bitcoin, right?"

Finch nodded and studied an eagle hovering over the shoreline. "Yeah. Four hundred and fifty million dollars worth simply vanished from a bitcoin exchange in Japan called Mt. Gox." He'd also interviewed two hedge fund managers caught up in the swindle. Three weeks later, one of them, Helmut Naumann had committed suicide in his office in Berlin. "I did the second interview with Toeplitz just before the trial began," he continued. "Toeplitz was trying to get me to publish a PR spin job. He was pretty upset when he realized I didn't spin it the way he hoped." Finch smiled, thinking about how he'd exposed the corruption at the heart of the senator's company.

Jennie set her hands on her hips and looked into the distance. "So that was Toeplitz."

"Yup. That *was* Toeplitz." But there was more to add. The story had occupied the press for a good three months, then moved to the back pages during the trial delays before it almost disappeared. "But two or three weeks before he died, the DA announced that Toeplitz had substantial incriminating evidence in hand and would testify *against* Whitelaw, Whitelaw & Joss."

Jennie focused her eyes on the tree limbs overhead. She appeared to be considering a distant problem, an anomaly. "So when exactly did the DA announce that he'd turned Toeplitz for the prosecution?"

Finch shrugged. "I'd have to check the files." In fact, he'd been off the case at the time, bouncing off the walls at Eden Veil, pondering how and when he'd crawl back to reality.

A puzzled look crossed her face. "And between the DA's announcement and last Saturday, what made Toeplitz drive through the Oregon switchbacks?"

"I asked Sheriff Gruman the same question." He'd been waiting to flash Gruman's name onto her radar, just to test her reaction, but she made no response at all. A real pro, he concluded, and decided to press on. After all, he'd given her a fair amount of info, now it was her turn to deliver. "What about the Mercedes? Bob Wriggly says Sheriff Gruman refused to classify the case as a crime without any substantiating evidence, but you insisted Wriggly had to keep the car secured."

Jennie looked away. Finch could tell that she was trying to determine if she could trust him.

"What about the car? Did you see it?"

More questions from her, but no answers. "I saw it," Finch said and nodded his head, a move to suggest this cat-and-mouse game had to end soon. "Just from a distance. Bob Wriggly wouldn't let me any closer. From what I can tell, the sheriff wants to move on, but you just want to *hang* on. Now why is that, Ms. Lee?"

"Why? Because I'm not ready to sign off on this one. Not yet. But I'll tell you when I am." She narrowed her eyes and stared at him. A long pause held between them, but Finch knew enough to let it linger. Finally she spoke: "There's something wrong with the blood."

"Something *wrong* with the blood?"

"Look, I'm sure you know how rare bear attacks are. Especially fatal attacks like this, with the victim secure *inside* his car. I don't think it's ever happened before." She rolled her lower jaw from side to side. "Beyond that, there's blood everywhere. It's like he bled out *inside the car*," she said and fixed her eyes on Finch again. "Look you can't print that. Not until I know for sure."

"What are you suggesting? I thought Ethan and Ben Argyle found the bear feeding on Toeplitz's corpse on the roadside."

"I know that."

She crossed her arms again and he realized he was only one or two questions from blowing the interview and losing Jennie as a primary source. He scanned the river below. The blood loss was vital information, whatever it meant. Depending on her final report, something explosive could emerge. He understood that if he released the news before she was certain, she could be compromised. But he needed answers.

"All right. I'll hold off on any mention about the blood until you're certain. But I've got to file a story tonight. And I'll report that the Mercedes is 'unofficially' impounded. That's information I uncovered on my own. In return for holding back your concern about the blood loss, I want to be the first reporter to read your final evaluation. Deal?"

She nodded with a look of determination. "All right, deal. But I need your help, too. I know you're going to pull this story apart any way you can. That's something I *can't* do because I have to live and work here. And you might stumble on some facts. I'd appreciate it if you tell me anything before you publish it."

A blank check. Finch had learned long ago never to negotiate an open-ended contract with a source. It gets far too complicated. "Look, Jennie, I can't open the door that wide because I don't know what's on the other side. And besides, just like you, I'm bound by professional ethics. And I never reveal my sources. For the same reason, I'd never reveal you as a source." He dropped his hands to his side, palms open, a plea for clemency.

"All right." She nodded. "But apart from those limitations, I want details from you."

"Agreed. And I'll let you know exactly when the DA flipped Toeplitz as a witness for the prosecution."

Finch smiled and held out a hand. She shook it firmly and without another word she turned and jogged west along the trail. He headed back towards his car. It'd be a grueling half hour walk without any stops to admire the scenery. With luck he could make it to Astoria High School before three o'clock.

※

Finch pulled the Ford Tempo to the side of the road and turned to the boy. "Is this about where it happened?"

"I think so." Ben Argyle tugged the earbuds from his ears and turned his attention to the gravel road ahead. He paused a moment to consider his surroundings. "The Mercedes was maybe twenty feet ahead and the bear itself another fifty yards or so."

The drive wasn't quite as arduous as Finch had anticipated. However, the time they saved driving up the switchbacks through the forests below Saddle Mountain was lost in the hour-long agreement he had to negotiate with Ben's father in the cafeteria at Astoria High School. Since Ethan Argyle didn't know Finch from Charles Manson, Finch asked Wally Gimbel to call Ethan immediately. Gimbel quickly verified his reporter's credentials and explained the urgent need to drive to the exact spot where Toeplitz had died. To further calm Argyle's anxiety, Gimbel faxed a testimonial from Lou Levine, Parson Media's attorney, to the high school. Finch also pledged to deliver the boy to his front door by seven o'clock so that he could eat dinner and bike over to his weekly scout meeting. Furthermore, Finch agreed to pay Ben a guide fee of fifty dollars. But what finally cinched the deal was Ben himself and the notion that two or three hours spent leading Finch through the gravel roads could count as his community service grad requirements.

"That'd seal it, Dad. I'd be done for the year," he'd said as if he'd found a dodge out of a long-dreaded school assignment.

Ethan narrowed his eyes, nodded and shook Finch's hand. "Okay."

Finch set the handbrake on the car, opened the door and grabbed his courier bag from the backseat and slung it over his shoulder.

"All right. Let's have a look," he said and he stood for a moment to take in the surroundings. The crispness of the air hit him immediately. At once he felt braced with a sense of renewed fitness, yet utterly lost in the wilderness. Perched beside the car, he tilted his head toward the sun — at least toward where he figured the sun ought to be — somewhere above the blankets of clouds crawling eastward overhead.

D. F. Bailey

"I didn't think it was supposed to rain that much way up here," he called into the car. When Ben failed to respond Finch walked to the passenger door and opened it for the boy. "Can you walk me through it?"

"I'll try." He curled his lips doubtfully and stepped beside Finch. Ben was a few inches taller than Finch, and like a lot of seventeen-year-olds, lean and unsteady. He looked as if he might teeter over at any moment.

"We came off that hill," he said and pointed to the ridge where his father had led them down to the road. Then he swung back to the gravel track and pointed with his left hand. "We saw the Mercedes right there."

"All right." Finch walked forward but the boy failed to keep up.

Finch had worried about this. While Ben had stowed his books in his school locker, the father revealed that his son might be too shaken to do anything more than point a way through the maze of switchbacks. The sight of Toeplitz's corpse "shook him badly," he'd said, but conceded that if Ben "could shoot a black bear when I'd missed my shot, then he can make his own decision about guiding you up there." True enough, during the drive along the mountain roads, Ben barely moved except to hand-signal left and right through the labyrinth that climbed ever higher.

"So where were you when you first sensed something was wrong?" Finch spoke in a very low tone and gently waved a hand, a gesture to bring Ben beside him.

Ben moved forward until they were about five feet from where the Mercedes might have stood. Then he moved a little to the left. "We could see the window was wide open. And the bear nuzzling something another fifty yards ahead."

Finch walked forward to where the passenger door would have been. "So did you look inside?" He leaned forward as though he could be peering into the SUV.

Ben pressed his lips together. "For just a second. Mostly it was Dad who checked it out."

"And then?"

"Then we saw the bear making moves."

"Just up there?"

"Yeah. That's where we shot at him. I was standing right here."

Finch watched as Ben anchored his feet in the ground. Clearly he was re-living the worst memories of the episode.

"Then your father took a shot and you took another. One shot each, right?"

"Yes, sir."

"And you hit his foot, you think. His right front paw?" Finch had already heard the story from Ethan Argyle, but he wanted Ben to confirm the details.

He nodded. "I know I hit him," he managed to say.

Finch squinted and tried to imagine the scene. But in the gray air all he could make out was the low scrub brush on the side of the gravel road and the still hills rising from the ravine. Very little suggested life of any kind, let alone death and dismemberment.

"Let's have a look," Finch said, sensing the boy's unsteady wavering. Perhaps he should simply move forward a step at a time.

"Sir, I don't think — "

"Just up here, you say." Finch forced a smile to his lips. Easy, steady, calm, he told himself. Just take the boy at his own pace.

"If you don't mind, I'm just going to wait in the car." He turned and then added, "You don't have to pay me if you don't want."

"All right." Finch nodded and released a heavy sigh. "Don't worry, I'll pay you. I appreciate you getting me up here, Ben. Good job." As he headed up the road he heard the car door close and the locks click into place.

Finch soon found the spot where the bear had mauled and devoured Toeplitz. The dried mud captured a record of events. He pulled his phone from his pocket and took a three-sixty video of the entire site, turning slowly on the spot. He reviewed the video to confirm that it provided a clear context of the scene, and then took a series of single-image shots. The gravel had been swept aside and a dark smear blotted the edge of the road. He sat on his haunches, patted the stained earth with the palm of his hand, held it to his nose and inhaled. Blood? There were very few other tracks visible in the grade and he could see the heavy tire imprint from the ambulance that had wound its way up here, turned, backed in and wheeled about. He heard a dry rattle as a light wind picked through some of the scrub. Beside him a trail of broken stems and branches led down the ravine. He took several more pictures, stood and walked a few feet along the ridge where the wounded bear must have tumbled downwards.

He walked back to where the Mercedes had been parked

and studied the terrain. He could see a second set of heavy prints embedded in the road. Likely the tracks from the Mercedes shackled to Wriggly's tow truck as they moved. His eyes found a pattern: forward, back, wheel around and exit. After capturing a few more images on the phone, Finch walked from the roadside into the tall weeds. There, laying at his feet gleamed a piece of brass. The shell casing from a spent round. He drew a latex glove from his bag, yanked it over his right hand and examined the brass carefully. He took three steps backward and there, smiling brightly at him, sat a second brass bullet shell. Two of them, likely from the Argyles' rifles. He placed the brass in a ziploc baggie that he carried for just such occasions and slipped it into his courier bag. Feeling a renewed vigor, he decided to scour the area by walking in a spiral pattern that widened from where the Mercedes had been parked over to the weeds on both sides of the road.

When he determined that no more information could be recovered from the site, he pulled the rubber glove from his hand, unlocked the car, dropped his courier bag in the rear footwell of the Tempo, sat in the driver's seat and stared through the window. Only one question remained unanswered: what had become of the bear? Beside him Ben appeared to sleep, his head buried in the furrows of his hoodie, pressed against the passenger window. Without waking the boy, Finch started the engine and began the drive back to Astoria.

Once he'd found the way to the highway, far from the remote site of primitive horror, he knew the boy would come around. That's when he'd ask him about the bear, allow Ben to unfold the story from a hunter's perspective, express his awe of the powerful forces he'd had to contend with: five or six hundred pounds of untamed, malevolent fury swerving toward him. Finch would ask him to tell every hunter's favorite story. About the one that got away.

※

After they emerged from the hills and re-entered the cell phone grid, two text messages pinged into Finch's phone. One from Fiona Page, the other from Bethany Hutt. Both texts demanded the same thing: "Call me."

Before he called anyone, Finch decided to take Ben to the local McDonald's, buy him a burger and milkshake and then drop him off at his home. Finch had Ben call his father to assure him that he wouldn't have to rush his son through dinner so that he could make it to the scout hall on time.

"Are you an Eagle scout?" Finch asked as they settled into the plastic booth with their food trays.

"Since last month." He took a bite out of his Quarter Pounder BLT and chewed it in silence.

Finch nodded and sipped his Coke and picked at some fries. He set aside the Filet-O-Fish he'd bought, thinking he'd save it for later. "Me, too," he said and thought back to his own adolescence. Scouts was an anchor for him during a turbulent period in his life. "In Montreal. My mother was French-Canadian, my dad was from New Jersey. So in Canada, Eagle scouts are called Queen scouts."

"Same in England," Ben muttered between chews. "It's from Lord Baden-Powell. He started scouts."

"That's right." Finch nodded to acknowledge this bit of arcane history. "Then when I was your age, we moved back to

New Jersey. The scouting skills were useful, too. I can't count the number of times I used them when I was in Iraq."

"You were in the army?"

"Public Affairs specialist," he said. His standard cover story.

"What's that?"

"It's like journalism, except in reverse."

"What?"

"Instead of the news, you report the messages the military wants everyone to hear." Finch shook his head to allay any more questions. Then he decided to add, "I met the President through that job. I actually shook his hand."

The boy stopped his near-compulsive eating. "Really?"

Finch nodded and then stopped himself. He wasn't fond of rose-colored autobiography. His four years in public affairs helped him enter and then graduate from Berkeley's journalism school. From there he talked his way into a job as a copy editor at the *San Francisco Post*. Only then did he feel like he'd landed on his feet. Just in time to secure a front-row seat where he could witness the slow-motion implosion of the print journalism world.

When Ben finished the burger Finch leaned forward slightly. "Hey, I was wondering. What kind of rifles were you and your dad using up there?"

Ben drew a long pull on the milkshake and nodded. "Dad has two Winchester 70s. Inherited from Mom's side of the family."

Those would account for the brass, Finch thought. "You didn't have any semi-automatics?" If Gruman was right and the

Argyles were preppers or survivalists, they'd certainly be warehousing something like a semi-automatic Bushmaster 15 — the weapon of choice for mass murder across the nation.

"Dad keeps them locked up. But when we're stalking deer, we just use the bolt-action rifles. Dad says one shot trains you to focus."

Deer stalkers. He smiled and thought of Sherlock Holmes's cap. "Old school, huh?"

Ben nodded and finished his milkshake, wiped his lips with a paper napkin and leaned against the bench. "Thanks," he said and smiled.

When they reached Ben's home, Will cut the ignition and studied the modest bungalow. "Look, Ben, I appreciate all your help today. I really do. If you can think of anything having to do with that bear or Mr. Toeplitz, I'd appreciate it if you'd contact me. I'm staying at the Prest." He handed him a business card. "I just want the story I'm writing to have all the facts. It's about telling the truth. Scouts' honor." He raised the three-finger salute and forced a light laugh through his lips.

They walked to the front porch and Ben's father swung the door open. Either he'd just noticed the car pull up or he'd been waiting. The look on his face revealed that he expected some kind of report. Natural for a school teacher, Finch guessed.

"Ben did a fine job," he said as they stood at the front door. "We didn't take a single wrong turn the whole time, did we Ben?"

He nodded and turned to face his father. "He met the president," he said. "And shook his hand."

"Really?" Ethan Argyle didn't seem impressed.

Finch shrugged it off. "I fed him at McDonalds," he said as he handed Ben sixty dollars. "There's a little extra for putting up with all my questions." He traded a fist-bump with him, then the boy slipped past his father and disappeared into the dark hallway. Finch realized there were no lights on anywhere in the house. Must be a survivalist's sense of energy conservation. "By the way," he continued and held Argyle's eyes, "have you heard any news about that bear?"

"Nothing," he said and leaned heavily against the doorframe. "Ben nailed him right through the front paw so he's in no shape to kill on his own anymore. At some point, he'll nose around somebody's cabin looking for an easy meal. That's when we'll hear about it."

"I guess. Have you ever come across a situation like this with a bear? Hauling a man from his car?"

"No. But he could be sick. Rabies, maybe." He narrowed his eyes. "Besides, bears are totally unpredictable. Despite their size, they're not street smart, if you know what I mean."

Finch shook his head, no.

"Around humans. Unlike coyotes or raccoons, say, they haven't figured how to live with people." He held a fist to his mouth, coughed, and looked into the hallway.

Finch sensed that Ethan had little time for any more conversation. "I'm sure you're busy," he said. "Thanks for loaning me your son. He's a good kid."

Argyle smiled and eased himself away from the door frame. "Let me know if I can do anything more," he said and took a step into his house.

"Thanks." Finch paused. "By the way, can I give you my

cell number?" He handed him a business card. "Whenever he emerges, I really would like to know what the heck became of that bear." His eyebrows notched with an expression of antici-pation. He knew that whoever bagged the bear would contact Argyle, probably within a few hours.

Ethan Argyle took the card and studied it a moment. "Sure, I'll call you."

"Thanks again, Mr. Argyle." Finch departed with another scout salute, middle three fingers to the side of his brow, and climbed back into his car.

※

Will Finch sat in the Ford Tempo at the junction just off Navy Pipeline Road and chewed idly on his Filet-O-Fish. He didn't like to think about the number of hours he'd loitered in various cars to track down a story. During his first year on the job, he'd wait for one source or another, someone like Senator Franklin Whitelaw, to leave his home, or office, or girlfriend's apart-ment. Then Finch would stride up the sidewalk and buttonhole the unsuspecting quarry for a quote that he could use to frame an article. The tactic, known as "ambush journalism," worked best when you had fresh allegations of scandal in a breaking story, especially when a denial could be more damning than a confession. You'd prepare two questions and fire both barrels at once: "Senator, have you heard that your girlfriend says you're *not* the father of her baby? What does your wife have to say?"

Disgusted by such tactics, he soon moved on to more credi-ble journalism. Nonetheless, almost every story required pa-tience and an ability to play the waiting game. This time, however, Will wasn't waiting for a source to appear. He was waiting for one to *dis*appear. When he saw Bob Wriggly's rusting Ford Econoline slip past him and roll toward town, he scrunched the last of his fish burger in the paper wrapper and tossed it into the passenger footwell.

"Take your time, Bob," he whispered and he steered the Escort up the road, through the open gate and into Bob's property. He parked as close as he could to the front entrance of the auto shop where Toeplitz's SUV was stored. While he studied the property, the building, the dozens of wrecked cars littering the yard, he tugged on his latex gloves. Everything appeared much the same as it had earlier in the afternoon, except now the door to the shop was shut.

"Worried about break-ins way up here?" he said aloud. He tested the bolt mechanism of the front door. Locked.

Remembering the rear access to the building, Finch worked his way around the south side of the structure in the shade of the cedar forest that bordered the small acreage. When he reached the east side of the building he smiled. The back door stood ajar and with a light push of his hand it swung into the dark interior of the auto-body shop.

Finch drew a flashlight from his courier bag and clicked it on. He swept the light over the chain link fence where Wriggly had secured Toeplitz's Mercedes-Benz with a five dollar padlock. Before he stepped inside, he listened to the sound of the room. Apart from the dull hum of white noise coursing through the ventilating system, he heard nothing suspicious.

Satisfied that he was alone, he moved quickly past the tool racks to the steel box where he'd seen Wriggly store the key.

Inside, a shallow tray held a dozen candidates and he pushed his index finger through them hoping to spot the Ace brand embossed on one of the brass slugs. *Yes, that one.*

He took the key to the fenced gate and applied it to the lock. *Click.* He opened the shackle and walked back to the tool chest and returned the padlock key to the interior tray. Then he pulled his motel key from his pocket and walked to the area where he'd paced back and forth in front of the chain link fence as he interviewed Bob Wriggly. He spotted a gray asphalt shingle on the floor and tucked the motel key under the thin edge of the shingle.

After he swung the gate open, Finch walked past the front of the car to the passenger side and gazed through the shaded glass. With his flashlight held next to this shoulder, he began a careful investigation of the GLK.

He clicked the camera app on his phone and took a picture of the driver's door with the open window, then snapped six wide-angle shots revealing the full scale of the big car and the scrawl of bear claw marks scratched across the black paint beneath the driver's window. *Nature versus the machinery of mankind.* The image would make quite an impression on the *eXpress* website.

He moved closer to the SUV, took a breath and held his nose to the open window. He exhaled and tested the air with short, tight sniffs. The black leather seats, smeared with dried blood, exuded a heavy, sickly odor that drove his head backwards.

"Jesus," he yelped and took a step away from the car.

After a moment he held his breath again, dipped his head

back through the open driver's window and took a dozen quick shots, each with a slight variation of angle and depth. With every flash from the camera the horror of Toeplitz's death briefly flared back to life. Each shot blinded him and soon he couldn't see anything clearly.

He stood off-balance for a few seconds and tried to blink the residual flashing from his eyes. He stepped back toward the fence and leaned against the gatepost. As he wobbled half-blind in the darkness he heard the crunch of gravel grinding up the hill outside the auto shop.

Still wavering, he tucked the phone into his pocket and teetered past the gate and shut it in place. Then he heard the Econoline engine shudder to a halt and Bob Wriggly call into the yard. "Finch? You here, Finch?"

The latex gloves puckered under Finch's thumbs and fingers as he tried to clip the padlock shut. Exasperated, he tore the gloves from his hands and shoved them into his bag.

"Finch? That you in there?"

He heard the key clicking in the far door.

"Yeah!" Finch yelled. "It's just me!"

As the exterior door yawned open a wide blade of the evening light flew along the concrete floor and landed at Will's feet. Finally he snapped the padlock shank into its case. Then without looking at Wriggly, he bent forward and began to sweep the floor with both hands.

"Finch?" Wriggly studied him from the distance. "What're you doing?"

"Oh. Bob. Gee, I'm glad you're here." He glanced at Wriggly, then turned his attention back to the floor. "You haven't seen my key, have you? I think I lost my motel key when I was here."

"Your key?" As he stepped into the shop, Wriggly's head swept from side to side, assessing the tool racks and cases, the hoist, the SUV parked behind the chain-link fence.

"Yeah. Crazy, I know." His hand brushed against the asphalt shingle. "Oh crap, will you look at that. Here it is!" He stood up and presented the key dangling from its plastic fob. He brushed his free hand over his eyes in an effort to wipe the lingering blindness from his sight.

"Funny. I never saw that all afternoon."

"Yeah. Well, it was under this shingle." He kicked it away with his heel. "Must have fallen from my pocket with my phone. He pulled his phone from his pocket, then slipped it back into place.

Wriggly studied him in silence.

"Look. I'm sorry, Bob. When I realized you weren't here, I thought I'd come through the back door" — he swung an arm toward the open door — "without bothering you. Was that not okay?"

Wriggly inched forward. "No, that's okay, I guess." He waved a hand dismissively. "I guess I'd have done the same."

"Good. That's what I thought, too." Will smiled. "By the way. You were right about that." He crooked his thumb toward the SUV.

"About what?"

"The smell."

"Yeah?"

"I haven't smelled anything that bad since I toured an

abattoir in Fresno for a story on the meat industry."

A look of certainty crossed Wriggly's face: *I told you so.*

※

Before he called Fiona Page, Finch sat on the bed in his room at the Prest Motel, opened his laptop and typed a list of the key questions he'd encountered:

1. What was Toeplitz doing so far from home?

2. The open window in Toeplitz's Mercedes. WHY?

3. What's the conflict between Gruman and Lee?

4. What's holding Lee from pursuing her questions about the blood inside the Mercedes?

Except for the conflicting analyses of Toeplitz's car by Gruman and Lee, Finch couldn't build a story on any of these questions. Especially since Lee had negotiated a temporary off-the-record deal. After a full day of investigation, all he possessed was a fog of evasions from Gruman, some digital photos, and a few quotes from Wriggly that he could weave into a feature about Toeplitz's final minutes on this earth.

He leaned forward and typed the first two sentences of the story lead: *Astoria's medical examiner and sheriff cannot agree on the circumstances surrounding the grisly death of Raymond Toeplitz. Until they do, the Mercedes GLK in which he died in a remote Oregon forest will remain secured by a private towing contractor.*

A pretty sleepy opening. He could see Wally Gimbel instructing Jeanine Fix, the *SF eXpress* copy editor and web master to insert the story on the bottom of the home web page

D. F. Bailey

for a day and then shuffle it into the digital archive. He began to click through the images he'd taken in Wriggly's garage and up in the hills, scanning them quickly to determine if any of them could be pimped into making a picture that Jeanine could use. He settled on the wide-angle shot of the GLK, the window still wide open — and with it the pressing question that lingered in the minds of everyone following the story: Why did Toeplitz open the window as the bear approached? Finch decided to make that question the hook for the story and within ten minutes he'd written two hundred words that Wally could use.

He liked to write in ten or fifteen minute bursts, like a diver plunging into the ocean, forced under until a near-death intensity pushed him up for air. Then he'd read over the sentences he'd written, correct the typos and phrasing, and dive in again. After five or six submersions he'd have most of the story in hand. Then he'd take a longer break, walk around, drink some coffee, and plod through a final edit. When he was satisfied, he'd send the text through the pipe to Jeanine Fix.

First, however, Finch decided to call Fiona to see what she'd uncovered about the Whitelaws. Depending on what she'd pried loose — and he wasn't expecting much — Will could roll her paragraphs into his story and they'd share the byline.

"Okay, brace yourself," she said. He could tell she was at home as the incoherent banter of her son, Alexander, resounded in the air behind her. Finch had met the boy only once. He was a shaggy, rough-and-tumble three-year-old who reminded him of Buddy when he was still a toddler.

52

"All right I'm braced. Did you actually manage to get one of the Whitelaws to go on record about Toeplitz?"

"No. Because they're not in town. They're no longer in California." Finch could picture her face, the tight smile she displayed when she unearthed some facts that might reveal buried treasure.

"All right. You're teasing me. So where are they?" He stood up and paced between the bed and the TV unit.

"Teasing you am I? Mmm, that's good I think." She laughed and continued, "The whole family's in Cannon Beach. A resort town that's about twenty miles south of you."

"Cannon Beach? What are they doing there?"

"That's for you to find out. Anyway all eleven of them are up there, right down to the chef, the maid and maintenance staff."

Finch paused to consider this. On the way up to Astoria he'd passed Cannon Beach on Highway 101. A remote play land, which made it attractive to anyone hankering for some seclusion.

"Want to know how I know all this?" she asked without prompting. "I drove to the family estate up in the Berkeley Hills. The gardener had just unlocked the front gate to their compound, so I buttonholed him. A Mexican guy, Cesar Diaz. Good thing I speak a little Spanish. He told me everything."

Finch smiled. "Must be a new employee. Obviously no one's briefed him on the Whitelaw code of silence."

"Yeah. Then I went online to the Clatsop County property appraiser's website and searched the deeds listed under Whitelaw. Looks like the place has been in the family for seventy-plus years. So," she paused, "I have an address for you."

Finch found his pen and note pad, ready to take down the address. "Shoot."

"It's not so much an address, as a location: Lot 2, Section A. If you go online, you'll see it's south of the village, just before Tolovana Park. Google doesn't seem to have a street view, but it looks like it might be on a slope facing the ocean."

"Everyone with money faces the ocean here," he told her and slipped the notepad into his courier bag. "You know, this explains something important."

"What?"

"What Toeplitz was doing up here. He must have been meeting with Whitelaw." Finch realized that he'd have to rewrite his story to suggest that Toeplitz had a meeting with Whitelaw. He now had a probable solution to the question at the top of his list: What was Toeplitz doing so far from home? Answer: Meeting Senator Franklin Whitelaw.

"Of course." She considered the implications for a moment. "But after the prosecutor turned him, I assume he'd be fired from the firm."

"Yeah. Maybe that's why he's dead now."

"What does *that* mean?"

Finch stared at the wall. He couldn't unravel all the threads. Not yet. "Look, there's nothing concrete, but there're these … *circumstances*. For instance, Toeplitz car's been impounded by the medical examiner. And other things I'm not sure of."

"Oh."

"You're brilliant, Fiona. I hope you know that," he said and opened the laptop and clicked on the story file.

She laughed. In the background Alexander chirped playfully. "Mom always told me, if you can't be good-looking, then you gotta be good."

"She told you that?" Finch considered Fiona's situation. A smart, hard-working single mom who'd divorced her husband before his advanced obsessive-compulsive disorder drove her, and her son, into madness.

"Think she was onto something?" Her voice revealed that she half-believed it.

"Nonsense. You've got the *full* package, kiddo." He could tell she needed someone to give her a boost. He decided to play it up a little. Besides, he hadn't flirted with a woman in a long time. Over the phone it felt safe. "You're smart, funny *and gorgeous*. Never forget that," he said.

"You know when you were gone last month I asked around about you."

"Oh yeah?" He sat on the bed and stared through the window. "And?"

"And there's a story about you in Iraq that just doesn't go away. So I figure part of it must be true."

"Which part?"

"The part about the prison in Abu Ghraib. The army torturing the Iraqi prisoners and how you broke the story."

"I didn't exactly *break* the story." He wove his fingers through is hair and recalled those weary days. He was twenty-four and completely over his head. *"60 Minutes* and *The New Yorker* did.* It was late April and early May, 2004."

"Most people here think you broke it."

"The truth is almost the exact opposite." He wanted to tell her the facts but he'd been sworn to secrecy. Instead, he relied on his usual explanation, the cover for his stint in Military Intelligence: "I was in the army, deployed in Baghdad with Public Affairs."

"*You* were a flack?"

"Before I saw the light, yes. That's what they called us." He laughed. "I was one a few guys who figured out Abu Ghraib. Let's just say I had the *inside story.*"

"And you passed it on to *60 Minutes?*"

He stood up, walked across the room and stood in the bathroom doorway. "You know, I should get going."

"Me too," she sighed.

"Don't forget what I said, okay." He tried to imagine her sitting at the dining room table in her apartment in San Francisco. Her dark hair would be down as she pulled it with one hand across her shoulder, her face looked clear but discontented. Standing in the Prest Motel next to the bathroom door in room 203, dreaming this image into his room, he blew a kiss into the phone and hung up.

Finch finished the rewrite and sent the story to Jeanine Fix. In a second email, he attached the photo of Toeplitz's car. Although it was a wide-angle shot, the mess of bear claw scratches etched across the black paint was clearly visible, and he advised Jeanine to write a caption that would lead the audience to inspect the damage the bear had inflicted on the vehicle. They could only imagine the horror Toeplitz had to face. An enticing news image drew readers into the story — made them want the picture *and* a thousand words.

He sent another email to Fiona recommending that if someone wasn't already on it, she should pitch a story to Wally: a background feature on bear attacks in general with a profile of black bear, versus brown bear, grizzly, and polar bear fatalities. From what he'd googled, he realized that while rare, almost every year two or three people were victims of horrible attacks. It wasn't his job to assign Fiona, or any other reporter, to the task but he hoped she'd grab the story so he'd have a single collaborator working with him inside the bog.

Job done, he propped himself on the pillows, tuned the TV to CNN and tapped the mute button on the clicker. He picked up his phone and checked the latest text from Bethany Hutt. Bethany was neither Will Finch's wife, nor Buddy's mother. But a month after they'd literally bumped into her in the dairy section of the Jackson Street Safeway, she adopted the role of wife *and* mother, which endeared her to both Will and his five-year-old son, Buddy. The two of them had lost Cecily to breast cancer a year earlier and Will realized that he and Buddy needed someone to embrace them both. Someone to smile the way Cecily had smiled. To look into Buddy's eyes and see him the way the boy's mother had seen him. Will knew that no one could replace Cecily, but Bethany made him imagine that *she* could. That she was the one.

Bethany had texted him every day since he'd signed into Eden Veil. Because he'd surrendered his cellphone the day they admitted him to the clinic, it wasn't until three weeks later, when he discharged himself, that he read the unbroken record of her desperation. Although this was shorter than all her previous texts (a simple plea: "call me") he deleted it, too. She blamed her disaster on Finch. Blamed her drinking on him, her depression, and the final, fatal car crash on him. In one brief flash she'd destroyed everything at the center of his life.

Once Buddy was gone, the only thing Finch could think to do was to destroy the last memory of *them*. All of them, Buddy included. That required a seventy-two-hour life course correction with a twelve bottle case of Dos Manos and some brand new friends that he met at Tres, a tequila lounge on Townsend Street near the Giants baseball stadium. Once the tequila was drained and all his money spent, two of his new pals kindly deposited him in a gutter next to the front tires of an SFPD squad car.

From that low and lonely patch of broken concrete his recovery began. After two days in the drunk tank, a brief court appearance (and five-hundred dollar fine), Finch walked back to his office, requested a medical leave from Wally, and signed himself into The Eden Veil Center for Recovery. To some of the residents, Eden Veil was an alcoholic rehab program. To others a general-purpose addictions recovery center.

To his surprise, Finch emerged in better shape than anyone imagined possible. He realized that, unlike Bethany, he wasn't an alcoholic. The visceral compulsion to drink didn't course though his blood. He had no nostalgia for the glorious binges of his youth. They simply didn't exist.

Tequila had provided the key to unlock Bethany's sexual inhibitions and it became part of their daily ritual. After two or three months, the ritual was reduced to drinking only. With Bethany now out of the picture he had no live-in drinking partner and no motivation to drink. In fact, drinking seemed like a manifestation of boredom. Or worse, self-loathing. Instead of all that, he discovered something deeper, that something more haunting gripped his soul: the hand of bereavement, with its chokehold of unremitting emotional loss.

At first he turned away from this realization. Then he learned an indispensable, primary lesson: *never run from emotion.* Better to look it in the face — whatever it is: love, fear, jealousy, *loss* — stare it down and embrace it. The insight occurred during the second week of his stay, when he was forced to confront the possibility that he might not be strong enough to address the death of his son.

"So if it's not alcohol that brought you here, it's something else." Dr. Michael Petersen, the senior therapist at Eden Veil, offered this conclusion after Will dismissed the notion that he was alcoholic.

Finch rolled the palm of one hand under his chin and looked away. They sat alone in Petersen's office, a windowless cube off the corridor of the center's second floor. A bare, mute space that inspired introspection.

"I guess," he said.

"Your son." Petersen's eyebrows wove together. "Buddy."

Will glanced at Petersen and nodded. He hadn't yet spoken Buddy's name aloud. He felt as if the sound of the child's name coming from his own mouth could somehow amplify the pain of his loss. "Something like that," he said when the silence between them deepened.

"Something like that, but *not* that?" Petersen drew himself up in his chair and leaned forward. "I'm going to guess that it's not losing Buddy that brought you here, but *the fear of embracing his death.*" He spoke these last words slowly, in a low pitch meant to penetrate Will's resistance.

What was he saying? Will dragged his eyes across the floor. Was it fear that had shaken him so badly?

When Finch failed to respond, Petersen continued. "Maybe you're afraid to acknowledge your responsibility in Buddy's death."

"*My* responsibility? I wasn't even there." He could feel his heart racing. What was Petersen trying to say?

"No. You weren't." Petersen's voice softened slightly. "I'm not saying it's your fault. Nobody's *blaming* you. But I want you to acknowledge the extent of your responsibility."

Finch stood up and paced behind the chair. He could feel the blood pulsing through his arms and chest. "My *responsibility* was letting Bethany into our home. And then letting my son get into my car with her. *When she was fucking plastered.*"

"Okay. That's it, then. That's the part you have to embrace. You have to look at what you allowed Bethany to do. What *you* helped her do."

Will's lips pushed down into a frown. He nodded and gasped for air. The room was compressing him, pressing his muscles and bones against its flat walls. "All right!" he shouted — and suddenly he was released.

"All right?"

"Yeah, I can *accept that,*" he said, not sure what exactly this might mean. "Accept that I let her into our lives. That I let her *destroy* us." He brushed his hands against his eyes. *Oh God, why is this so hard?*

"Easier said than done." Petersen eased back in his chair. "You've got to actualize that, man."

"You think this is easy?"

"No, I don't. I think this is the hardest thing you've ever tried to do." From his desk drawer Petersen lifted two mini José Ceuvro tequila bottles into his hand, the one-point-seven ouncers served on airplanes. As he dangled them in the air, the liquid gold shimmered under the fluorescent lighting. "What's the most important thing you *lost* from drinking?"

Finch rolled his lips and cast his mind inward. The answer was obvious but he couldn't say it.

"What was the one gift that booze ripped out of your life," Petersen said in a whisper. But he didn't pose it as a question. More a statement of fact.

Finch rolled his head from side to side. This was hard. Hard to feel. Hard to confess that he'd lost so much.

"Buddy," he said at last and glanced at Petersen, then at the polished linoleum floor. "*Losing* Buddy," he said firmly, as a point of clarification.

"So, finally. Do you realize that's the first time I've heard you speak his name?"

A dark look crossed his face, a new tinge of shame. "No."

Petersen nodded and set the two bottles of tequila on his desk. "You got a picture of him?"

Finch nodded again. "Back in my room."

"Let's go." Petersen tucked the bottles into his pocket and led them out of his office, up the stairs to the resident dorms that looked onto the park.

Finch pawed through his dresser and handed Petersen the

three-by-four inch picture of Buddy and Cecily sitting on a bench at the zoo. He perched on his dorm bed and studied Petersen's face.

"Who's the woman?"

"My wife, Cecily. Buddy's mom." Will tried to smile. "She passed almost two years ago."

"He was a nice looking kid, Will."

Petersen was one of the few people who knew the background story. About the afternoon when Bethany attempted to drive Buddy to his T-ball game, after Finch had told her to wait until he'd finished repairing a tire on Buddy's bike. He'd told her that he — *Will* — would drive him, and then ten minutes later it registered that she hadn't waited and they'd left without him. At the same time, perhaps at that very moment, she smashed his Toyota — and Buddy — into the concrete on-ramp leading onto the 101 from Market Street.

"I want you to try this tonight, before you go to bed." Petersen drew the two tequila minis from his pocket and stood them on the night table next to Finch's bed. Then he slipped the picture of Buddy between the two bottles.

The two men studied the arrangement he'd made, a miniature shrine built of liquid gold and grief. For a moment Finch felt like smashing it to the floor, smashing Petersen for being a probing piece of shit. Then he realized that Petersen was right. This make-shift memorial was a reminder of Finch's lapse, a chapel where he could worship his son's memory. Alcoholic or not, he needed to embrace this new chastity. It was a way to honor his love for Buddy and Cecily, to embrace them both again.

Remembering all that, remembering his life with Buddy and Cecily, Finch now reached into his courier bag and took out the small leather case where he stored Buddy's picture and the two mini-bottles of José Ceuvro and set them on the night-stand beside his bed in the Prest Motel. He washed up, then pulled the bedcovers open and lay down, clicked off the TV and the night lamp. He didn't need to think about booze or Bethany too often anymore. He was almost past all that, and he knew it. But Buddy and Cecily he would always remember.

Finally he set those memories aside, too; instead he considered the questions he'd put to Franklin Whitelaw tomorrow. Questions for the Senator's sons and wife and daughters, or anyone else willing talk to him about Toeplitz.

CHAPTER FIVE

Thursday morning, as Finch stood under the shower in his bathroom at the Prest Motel he tried to assess where his story was headed. Obviously there was more to Toeplitz's death than Sheriff Gruman let on. Jennie Lee was confident of that, but because she had no solid evidence of foul play, she was temporarily blocked by Gruman and had to bide her time. But soon her hand would be forced by Toeplitz's estate lawyers and unless she made a formal request for an investigation, his car would be released, cleaned and repaired, and any forensic evidence destroyed. Finch also had other concerns. Ben Argyle's immobilizing panic up in the mountains seemed far too extreme for such an accomplished kid. Was there more to his anxiety than he'd revealed? The question hung in Finch's mind, another tiny piece in a jigsaw puzzle without any edges.

There seemed to be more tangents to the story than anyone imagined. He knew that playing ball on visitor's turf held a distinct disadvantage and that he needed as many allies as he could gather. If he could gain his trust, Ben Argyle might disclose what was really troubling him. But Finch's first recruit had to be Jennie Lee, so after his breakfast he sorted through the electronic files that Fiona had sent to him and when he found what he needed, he composed an email to Jennie that would demonstrate his good faith and build on their agreement:

Jennie, thanks for meeting with me yesterday.

As promised, I've unearthed the timing of the DA's announcement that he'd bring Toeplitz to the stand for the prosecution: May 4 at 2 PM. Five days later — on May 9, the Argyles came across Toeplitz's corpse. Working backward, assuming he'd died the previous day, that makes the date of his death May 8. Assuming at least a day to drive from San Fran to Astoria (it took me just under 12 hours) and another to pack his bags, etc., that puts his departure from SF no later than May 6. In other words, he died within 48 hours of arriving in the county.

I don't know if you've heard this, but the Whitelaw family spent the past week in their compound in Cannon Beach. That suggests to me that Whitelaw called Toeplitz in on short notice — which explains why Toeplitz was here at all. Whitelaw's motive? A last chance to turn Toeplitz away from the DA and back to the firm's cause? And Toeplitz's motive? So far, I can't imagine why he'd want to cross swords with Whitelaw following the DA's announcement. That's one thing I want to unearth when I pay Whitelaw a visit this morning.

I'll call you when I know more. I'd also like to hear your findings at the end of today.

By the way, any news of the bear?

Best, Will.

The drive south along Route 101 gave him about forty minutes to prepare for Whitelaw. For any interview that's destined to be adversarial, he'd learned to arrive on the scene unannounced. The only two advantages a reporter possesses are physical and psychological surprise. Physical surprise means you materialize as if sent by God. Your abrupt appearance can create a lapse, a sort of forgetfulness, and before the interviewee remembers to tell you to bugger off, he's already answered three or four questions. The second surprise is psychological. Your questions spear directly to a critical point, to the need-to-know answer your story hangs upon. But no matter what, at some juncture the impact of surprise will diminish and you'll be tossed out the door and the interview is over. Never expect a second chance. And if you're facing a media veteran, sometimes the end of the interview can arrive at the moment of confrontation. Once you hear the word "trespass" you're legally advised to back away. If you hesitate, as Finch had learned on two separate occasions, you can expect a punch to the nose. A sorry way to ruin an otherwise agreeable day.

The drive through the village of Cannon Beach was pleasant enough. The tidy shops and cottages were all clad with clapboard and shingle siding, some painted a traditional Cape Cod gray, but many were left unpainted and exposed to the salt and wind that rolled up from the expansive beach to the west. The ocean seemed to lick at the low-lying town, renowned for its vulnerability to a tsunami that, when it arrived, would sweep the village into the forests on the east side of Route 101 and then rip and splinter whatever remained as the waves rolled back into the sea.

As he drove past their driveway, Finch realized that Fiona's description of the Whitelaw beach estate understated the invisibility of the compound. While there was no gate to control traffic into and out of the property, a long gravel driveway climbed a steep hill overlooking the road and ocean. Somewhere above him, well beyond the reach of any tsunami, the property stretched back into the forest. Finch parked his car on the shoulder of the road where it widened above a reinforced bank. He trod up the hill, turned a corner and an outbuilding appeared on the right. The property manager's house, he supposed. Behind it stood the main building, a three-story wood-framed hunting lodge that combined all the essentials of luxury fused with rustic domesticity. Anyone could tell at a glance that Senator Franklin Whitelaw had successfully combined two mainstays of west coast Americana: an enterprising spirit and cash.

On the left stood a four-bay garage. Like all the other buildings, it was faced with rough-hewn cedar planks, left unpainted so that over the years the ocean winds and rain had weathered them to the natural colors of the landscape. One garage door was drawn up, revealing a red Mercedes-Benz C320 Sport Coupe. Much sexier than Toeplitz's GLK, but probably too sexy for Franklin Whitelaw himself. Fiona was right again: likely his sons and daughters were here, too. The whole family gathered for consultation in the face of a potentially devastating law suit — and Toeplitz called in for one last chance to save himself. Or die.

No one was visible on the front yard, a patchy mix of turf and compacted sand, impossible to cultivate into anything

D. F. Bailey

resembling a lawn. Even this far back from the shore, the winter storms would smash into this piece of paradise with sheets of sand blown up from the miles of uninterrupted beach below. Before he continued, Finch turned to admire the view. In the distance, groups of families and partying teenagers had planted umbrellas next to the shoreline and unloaded food and beverages from their ice chests: Perrier and brie, pinot noir and grilled asparagus tips. Rising from the shallow foreshore, a massive boulder, Haystack Rock, appeared on the right. The entire effect was picture perfect.

Finch approached the front door of the main building. Above the entrance hung a wooden sign with the word, SALVUS carved into the plank. Latin for salvation. He wondered what sort of salvation Whitelaw and his clan might have in mind. He could make out the ring of laughter echoing from behind the house and decided to wander into the backyard, hoping to find the senator in an unguarded state of mind. When he turned past the kitchen he saw a tennis court, a professional-looking installation properly fenced with an elevated referee's chair perched above the net.

Four people in their mid-twenties, all dressed in tennis whites, were enjoying a set of mixed-doubles. In the ref's chair sat a brunette woman trading shouts with one of the men. Dressed in a black blouse and black skirt, she looked five years older than the players on the court. Various cat-calls and mock threats rose between their accusations and from time to time, the two girls on the court burst into laughter. Completely pre-occupied, none of them noticed Finch as he stepped into the shade of the roof gable above the kitchen wall. Suddenly the mock-argument turned with bitter seriousness.

"Jennifer, you witch!" The ref threw her sun visor to the ground, climbed down from her chair, stood on the clay surface with her hands bunched on her hips. Will imagined that she was about to punch her tormentor in the face. Then she turned and strode towards him.

"Gianna, come on. Stop it," Jennifer begged in a tone that resembled the earlier playfulness. "I know you're upset. I was just kidding for goodness sake."

"Please, Gianna," her male partner called. Finch recognized him; one of the Whitelaw boys. Medium height, medium build and medium looks compromised by premature balding. His brother stood facing him on the opposite side of the net. Their twin skulls were glowing in the brilliant spring sunshine.

"Yeah, Gi-Gi, we can't go on without you," his brother pleaded. "Not against these ivy leaguers. Without a ref, we all know they cheat!"

Finch stood motionless in the shadow, realizing that Gianna would soon cross in front of him as she approached the kitchen door. When she entered the canopy of shade, she took a step backward as if someone had pushed her shoulder.

"Whoa. You startled me," she said in a low voice to Finch. Despite the scare she seemed composed, indifferent to the taunts from the tennis players who resumed their game with a serious attitude.

"Sorry!" Finch held a hand aloft and forced a smile to his lips. "Silly of me. Happens all the time," he added and stirred his hand, waving away an imaginary bee.

"Me too," she said. "Skittish by nature."

"Runs in some families," he said and shifted gears to a conversational tone. "My mother, for example. Even though she *knew* she was an anxious person, it didn't help her to overcome it." He smiled. "She was nervous 'til the day she died."

"Right." Gianna studied him a moment and smiled. Although they'd never met, she appeared happy to see him. Someone to lift her out of the boredom of tennis. "And you're with *which* of my brothers?… "

He smiled again. "Oh, sorry. I'm Will Finch." He held out a hand to her.

"Gianna Whitelaw." She shook his hand with a surprising vigor and her mouth revealed a look of doubt. "Oh please. Don't tell me you're here with one of the *girls*."

He glanced at the girls as they skipped across the court. Healthy, lively, ripe. "No." He leaned toward Gianna and whispered, "Too young for me."

She seemed to like that, as though he'd turned a key that unlocked the door to her sense of trust. "Care to join me for a cocktail — or too early for you?" She led the way into the designer kitchen, a large room with restaurant-grade appliances: a six-burner gas cooktop with custom copper range hood, built-in refrigerator-freezer and dishwasher.

"Yeah." He tapped the face of his watch. "Too soon for me. But I see you've got some coffee on."

"Coffee's always on at this place."

"Great. Black, no sugar."

"Aren't you a hardy fellow." A blush rose through her neck and settled on her cheeks. Beneath the pink tinge he detected a Mediterranean richness in her skin. Deep, warm tones in her arms and taut calves below her skirt. She smiled and poured a mug of coffee for him.

They sat at an oak table next to the window, bunting small talk to one another. Finch decided to run with whatever entered her mind, and when the time was right, steer his way to the topic of Toeplitz. Now installed in her house, engaged in conversation, drinking with her, Gianna apparently assumed that he must be a party guest; his attachment to a specific brother or sister no longer interested her. She leaned toward him as she spoke and her black blouse dipped open revealing the tight cleavage of her breasts. Obviously a push-up job, he mused. But effective enough.

"You know, you remind me of him." Her chin dipped with a hint of sadness. "Your eyes."

"Remind you of who?"

She shrugged as if it should be obvious. "Raymond."

Finch blinked. In an instant several puzzle pieces locked together. Raymond Toeplitz — and her black blouse and skirt. She was in mourning. But none of the other tennis players were. If anything, they appeared to be celebrating. And their argument on the court wasn't about a disputed line call. It must be about the chasm that separated their lives with the deceased. But he had to test that idea before he continued.

"You mean Mr. Toeplitz." He offered this as statement, not a question.

"Of course." She hesitated at the formality. "Did you know him?" Her eyes narrowed as if she might be on the verge of linking him to someone in her world.

"Yes. We met twice." He broke eye contact, eager to find

71

another topic. "Oh … I'm sorry. I just realized … you're in mourning."

She took a long pull on her drink and set the glass on the table. "Fuck, someone has to bear his memory."

Finch shook his head. "But not the others."

She rolled her eyes in disgust. "What do the sports guys say? *One and done.* Well, one day they drove Ray out of here, and then … he was done."

"*Drove* him out of here?"

Before she could answer they were distracted by a rustling in the hallway off the kitchen. Then Finch heard footsteps approach. Senator Franklin Whitelaw entered the room, an open newspaper in one hand, reading glasses in the other. "Anybody seen the business section?" he asked.

A tremor rattled through his hand as he slipped the glasses into his shirt pocket. He set his eyes on Finch with a distant look. "Sorry, I don't think we've met. I'm Franklin Whitelaw. *Proprietor,*" he added with a brief laugh and swept his free hand across the room.

"Daddy, this is Will Finch."

He set the newspaper on the table and they shook hands. Finch realized that the senator didn't recognize him or his name. The advantage of surprise remained.

"He knew Ray."

"I heard the news early this week. On Monday," Finch said. "Sorry to hear about it. Quite a shock. I mean *what happened,*" he added to emphasize the bear attack.

Whitelaw's eyes swept the floor as if he were searching for something. "Unbelievable," he said. "Who ever thinks these things still happen?"

"I know. For the life of me, I can't figure out what he was doing up in the switchbacks. His car parked. The window *open*."

Whitelaw cocked his head. "Sorry — you *knew* Ray?"

"Briefly. We spoke a few times."

"And that was *how?*" His head ticked from side to side and he fixed his gaze on Finch.

"I interviewed him." He was about to be outed and knew that his only recourse was to come clean. "For the *eXpress*. I wonder if you could tell me when you last saw him."

Whitelaw seemed stunned, took a step backward and glanced at Gianna.

"Apart from the boys, who followed him up to Saddle Mountain, same as all of us," Gianna said as her father tried to determine who exactly was sitting at his table drinking his coffee. "The morning he died we were both standing right here, in fact." She pointed to the floor. "Except when Raymond put out his hand to say goodbye, Daddy, *you* wouldn't shake it." Her jaw wobbled and in a weak voice she added, *"Would you, Daddy?"*

"All right. Enough." He waved his hand in a motion to keep her in her chair. "Do you realize who you're talking to?!"

"Somebody who knows how to listen," she spat out. "For a *change!*"

"I said, *enough.*" Whitelaw's eyes narrowed and his body shook with a violent twitch.

Gianna wrapped her arms across her chest and her head sank a notch.

"Mister Finch, I want you out of this house immediately." He marched over to the back door. "I consider your presence here an unlawful trespass." He stuck his head out the door and called toward the tennis court. "*Justin. Evan. Get over here!*"

"Gianna, nice to meet you. You need anything, you call me. I'm at the Prest Motel." Finch gave her a business card and turned to Whitelaw. "There's no cause for alarm, Senator Whitelaw. I'm leaving now." He made his way to the kitchen door and eased past the senator. Whitelaw matched Finch's height, but the senator's frame was leaner and more taut due to the decades of his legendary running routine.

"I appreciate your help," Finch said as he looked toward the tennis court. The Whitelaw boys stood slack-jawed, tennis rackets dangling from their hands as they tried to make out who was standing in the kitchen shade.

"Everything I said — and whatever you heard from my daughter — is off the record. Do you understand that?" the senator barked.

"Now that you've requested it, from this moment on, yes," Finch said and clipped a parting salute to him. He rounded the corner and made his way to the front of the house. Two men were weeding the garden flower beds. He nodded at them and strolled down the gravel driveway toward his car. Fortunately, he didn't need any quotes on the record from Whitelaw. What he needed was facts. And now he had a fistful of them.

For the first time in weeks — since he'd checked out of Eden Veil — Finch felt completely alive. I'm back, he whispered to himself. *Back in the game.*

※

Five minutes later, as he entered the village of Cannon Beach, his phone rang. When Finch saw that the call was from Jennie Lee he pulled over in front of a gift shop on South Hemlock Street.

"Where are you?"

"Cannon Beach." He studied the shop window next to the car. "In front of a store selling what looks like varnished sea shells strung from hemp necklaces."

"Could be any one of a dozen." She laughed and shifted her voice tone. "Okay, a deal's a deal. You sent me the info from the DA's press conference and I promised you'd be first to read my report once I publish it."

"So it's out?"

"Not yet, but something's come up."

"You've got news?"

"More than news. We got the bear. Just below the Lewis and Clark River. About a mile from where they found Toeplitz's corpse. My guess is that the bear found a shallow cave or hollow tree and just went to ground."

Finch detected some warmth in her voice. She seemed more amiable on the phone than she'd been in person yesterday. Something had changed, but he had no idea what. "Are you sure it's the *right* bear?"

"I haven't seen it yet, but Manfred Dilkes said the top of the right front paw was shot through." She paused as if no further proof were needed. "We can verify it by the end of the day. I'll probably start the necropsy after lunch."

"Who's Manfred Dilkes?" Finch's eyes wandered the length of the street. Dozens of tourists slipped in and out of the cafés and shops.

"My autopsy technician intern. He usually handles our milk runs."

Milk runs. Obviously a trade euphemism for hauling in the dead and laying the cadavers onto a dissection bench.

"He took the call from another pair of hunters. They shot the bear this morning after it took a half-hearted run at them. I guess with his wound he hadn't eaten since Saturday."

Finch thought of Toeplitz. Neither of them wanted to bring up his name. Not in this context.

"Any chance I can sit in?" In all his years at the *San Francisco Post,* the medical examiners barred the press from their autopsy procedures. But never had a crime been linked to the death of an animal. Maybe the rules were different for necropsies.

"It's not normal," she said, "but with an animal it's not *technically* prohibited. I can see how it might be used as an education piece for the press. So I'm not —"

"I'll be there." He interrupted her before she could backtrack. "Just say when."

"Look ... it's not going to be pleasant." She paused so he could absorb this. "Just so you understand: I don't do necropsy hand-holding."

"No problem. I rarely do actual hand-holding of any kind." He laughed, tried to make this into a joke. "Just tell me where to show up."

"Normally wherever we find the animal. But since we need tissue samples to confirm a link to Toeplitz, I'll operate in the pit," she said. "Otherwise known as the medical examiners room."

※

The examination room was windowless, well-lit, clean — but not spacious. "The pit," as Jennie Lee called it, was located at the rear of the ground floor of Jennie's building. Two french-style, steel doors opened onto the driveway where a van could back in and unload the corpses entrusted to the medical examiner. At the center of the examination room lay a stainless steel bench the size of single bed. Surrounding the bench stood an array of open shelves, closed cupboards, surgical trays, audio and video recording devices. An integrated sink and tap were attached to the foot of the examination bench and tilted at a slight angle to create a gravity drainage system for disposable fluids. Of all the implements at hand, only the sink and tap made Finch shudder. He knew they were essential for procedural hygiene, but they suggested the finality of the whole business. He'd seen quite enough of this during his time in the army field hospitals in Iraq. The Astoria medical examination room reminded him of the lesson he'd learned overseas: death commands an endless tyranny.

For a moment he reconsidered Jennie's warning about hand-holding but she quickly had him suiting up in a plastic apron and pants. She then handed him a clear face mask. The plastic sizing strip on the back of the head band was identical to most baseball caps. He made a guess, snapped the strip into place and fitted the band around his head, with the shield peaked upward, open like a welder's hat.

"Okay. I want you to stand at the far end of the table. And keep out of our way." She turned to her colleague and nodded.

"Manfred, you ready?"

"You bet."

Manfred, a recent grad from Oregon Health & Science University had started an autopsy technician internship with Jennie in January. He appeared to be bright, focussed, eager. Finch wondered how long Manfred could maintain his sunny disposition for the job.

The intern led the way to a collapsed stretcher stowed next to the french doors. He clicked some hidden buttons that released four wheels under the accordion legs, heaved on one end — and suddenly the stretcher became a sturdy mobile unit that he ushered through the double doors. Manfred opened the rear of the van and the three of them worked together to slide the tarp supporting the bear onto the stretcher and then wheeled the cadaver back into the examining room. With another coordinated effort they angled the stretcher to a twenty-degree slope and slid the bear onto the examining table. The whole operation took less than five minutes. Considering the weight of the bear — he looked to be at least five hundred pounds — it was an impressive performance. Finch shut the double doors and watched as Manfred clicked the buttons again and shuffled the collapsed stretcher back into a storage locker.

Jennie turned on an overhead light and the bear immediately became the centerpiece of the room. She stepped over to a desk next to the wall, clicked on an audio recorder and spoke into a microphone suspended from the ceiling. "This is Jennifer Lee, Clatsop County ME, on Thursday, May 13 at 13:20 hours. Manfred Dilkes, ME intern, is attending." She paused, glanced at Finch and continued. "Mr. Will Finch from the *San Francis-*

co eXpress is observing. We're performing a standard necropsy procedure on an Olympic black bear — *Ursus americanus altifrontalis* — suspected of the fatal attack on Mr. Raymond Toeplitz on or around May 8."

As she completed a few tasks at the desk, Manfred used a steel tape to record several measures of the bear: length, girth, leg spans. He noted the weight, calculated by a scale built into the examining table. "Five hundred and eight pounds," he announced and raised his eyebrows in a pique of surprise. "I imagine he lost some mass over the past week."

"It depends." Lee turned her chin to one side. "If he was in shock, his metabolism could easily emulate the hibernation process. In which case he wouldn't eat or defecate."

"In which case," Manfred said as he looked at Finch, "the stomach contents should tell us something about Toeplitz."

Jennie hesitated and then approached the table. "Here's our sad friend." She cast her voice toward the microphone as she walked to the bear's side. She looked into his face and at his left shoulder which had absorbed a rifle shot a few hours earlier. Her gloved fingers explored the wound and after some initial probing, she inserted her index finger into the bullet hole. "One shot to the upper left shoulder. No exit wound," she announced. "Obviously a disabling shot." She focussed her attention on the massive head and turned the snout in her hand and leaned over to examine the back of his skull. "A second shot, fired into the forehead, with an exit wound directly opposite to the point of entry. Whoever put him down was humane about it."

Then with a tenderness that surprised Finch, she lifted his

right front paw in her gloved hands and examined the wound
inflicted by Ben Argyle's Winchester rifle. The paw was little
more than a torn piece of blood-matted fur clotted with green
pus.

She continued her recording: "The wound to the right front
paw is consistent with the claim from Ethan and Ben Argyle
that they injured the bear five days ago. The deterioration of
the exposed flesh and the state of infection on the site is also
consistent with their claim."

Finch stood in one corner of the room, mentally chronicling
the procedures. But now, above the sound of Jennie's clinical
assessment, he became aware of something new. He could
smell the bear. The damp odor of mildewed rot washed through
him in a wave. He was no longer watching the bear; instead,
the bear was invading him through Will's nose and mouth. He
gasped and drew a long breath and then stepped backward until
his shoulders rested against the wall.

"Mask," Jennie said and flipped the clear plastic shield into
place in front of her face.

With his eyes on Finch, Manfred slid his mask forward and
slowly shifted it back and forth, as though Finch needed a
demonstration of how to proceed. After a final adjustment he
set his face shield into place and began to assist Jennie.

Finch drew another breath and pulled the mask over his
face. The plastic shield covered him from his hairline to his
throat. Jennie had yet to make the first incision and he wondered if he'd be able to watch the entire procedure. He forced
his eyes to stare at the massive corpse on the examining bench.

"If you need to, go back through the door we came in. We

won't be more than twenty minutes," Jennie said looking at him. Her eyes reflected a concern that he might not hold up.

Finch nodded and without another word, Jennie drew a surgical saw from the tray beside her, clicked it on and under the whine of the saw she muttered something into the microphone above her head.

Twenty minutes, Finch thought. As he set his jaw, determined to see the necropsy through, he began to argue with himself, one part articulating how his presence was unnecessary to writing a decent report, the other part demeaning his mental weakness and insisting that a first-hand account would strengthen the story that he knew could be a critical part of Toeplitz's obituary.

He watched Jennie cut a line from the bear's chest down through the pit of his stomach to what Finch assumed was the pubic bone. Except for some clotted spatter, the cut was clean and bloodless. Perpendicular to the incision, she made two additional cuts, one on each side that opened the bear's slack belly. Manfred then applied two clamps to pull the carcass open and expose the bear's stomach and intestines. A new wave of terrible rot — the unmistakable stench of death — flooded through the room and into Finch's nostrils.

"We'll be quick now," Jennie said and proceeded to incise the bear's stomach.

In an effort to block the rank horror, Finch shut his eyes and began to debate the idiocy of his reaction. He'd witnessed so much living human horror in Iraq. How could a few incisions into a dead bear be so unnerving? He forced himself to stare into the eviscerated stomach, once again held open by

Manfred's expert use of surgical clamps. At first Finch couldn't make out what he was seeing. Then it came to him: the bear's last meal, mashed by his powerful jaws and partially digested over the last five days as his digestive system began to collapse.

Finch's head spun and he had no idea what the bits of exposed bone and flesh might be. He hoped that none of this could make any claim to Toeplitz, that what Manfred began to extract from the stomach was a collection of berries and fish, maybe a deer or several rats. On the other hand, Finch knew that soon Jennie and Manfred would take this sordid collection and test it against the DNA samples they'd collected during the Toeplitz autopsy.

He pressed the back of his head to the wall. He now stood rod-straight in the corner of the room, as far as possible from the examining table. But the room was so compact that he could clearly see everything that Manfred laid in two stainless steel pans between the bear's outstretched legs. Finch could feel his stomach rising, a wedge of his own undigested food, knotted and climbing steadily toward his throat. He drew another long breath through the mask and forced himself to step away from the wall. *Stand tall, damn it.*

"Well, look at this," Jennie said and lifted something into one gloved hand. "Hello. What have we here?"

"And here's another," Manfred said and pinched a pellet between his right thumb and index finger. "What are they?"

Jennie took the object from Manfred and held both slugs against the light. She studied them a moment. "They look like small caliber bullets. Check the carcass again, Manfred. Maybe we missed some entry wounds."

She inserted her hand into the exposed belly again. This time she extracted a third object, another oval, and held it to the light. Finch was transfixed by the opaque, gelatin ball.

"Oh dear," she whispered. "It's a human eye."

These were the last words Finch could make out. At the same moment that Manfred Dilkes turned to re-examine the carcass for entry wounds from the new-found bullets, Finch crashed into the autopsy technician's arms and broke his fall. A second later he pitched forward onto the concrete floor in a dead faint.

✳

"Manfred gave you a five-point-five." Jennie turned her head to one side and frowned with a look of doubt. "Sorry, but I have very strict standards. I could only go as high as a four-oh. That's out of ten, by the way." She smiled again, a look that forced Finch to turn away. He shook his head with embarrassment.

In the moments after they'd stripped the mask from his face and dragged Finch through the examining room into her office, apparently Manfred and Jennie had assigned olympic-point scores to the reporter's sudden pirouette and collapse at their feet. Jennie had taken the trouble to wipe his mouth and nostrils to ensure his airways were clear before she snapped a vial of smelling salts under his nose. Manfred then propped him in a chair with his head slung between his spread knees, and they told him to stay put while they completed the necropsy on their own. Fifteen minutes later Jenny returned to the office, took his pulse and blood pressure, determined that he was fit to drive and told him to meet her at Three Cups Coffee House in an hour.

When Finch opened the door to the café he spotted her sitting next to the windows at the far end of the room, one table away from where he'd sat with Sheriff Gruman. Finch, still feeling the knot of food in his belly, bought a cup of tea and joined her.

"Maybe you can give me another chance to better my score," he said, certain that the only way to save face was to play along. "Next time I'll stand on the lip of the examining table. Then make my move."

"Uh, noooo." She waved a finger. "Sorry, that was a one-time trial with permanent disqualification."

"What?" He sipped his tea and set the cup aside.

"Sorry." She tipped her head and her attitude shifted to a more serious tone.

"All right," he conceded. "But tell me, did the DNA match Toeplitz?"

She rested her chin in the palm of one hand and nodded. "No surprise, really."

"Jesus." Finch glanced away. "What about the two bullets you found?"

"What bullets?"

Again Finch turned his eyes away. He stared at the Columbia River passing under the long bridge. *So, we're back to playing games with one another.* Finch held up a hand, cop-style, bringing a line of traffic to a halt. "Sorry, Jennie, but with every second step forward I feel as though I have to negotiate the ground rules with you."

She took a sip of her coffee and sat back with arms folded. "Why? I was the one who called you about the bear. *And* let you sit in on the necropsy. Do you think I always do that?"

He studied her a moment. "Look, I have a story to write. And you're probing a case that we both know isn't exactly what it seems."

"So what is it, *exactly?*" She uncrossed her arms and leaned forward. A self-assured look came over her face.

"I'm talking about those two slugs you found in the bear," he said with a gasp of exasperation. "Look, forget about all that for now. What matters more is that you're obviously afraid of something. Maybe you're afraid of over-stepping your bounds. Maybe it's your boss. Who do you report to anyway?"

"Officially, Oregon's chief medical examiner. But in a town this size … practically speaking? Gruman." She rolled her lips together and looked away.

"And you already had a little tug-of-war with him over the disposition of Toeplitz's car."

She nodded as if, with some patient prodding, she could add more details, but then Manfred Dilkes appeared at the restaurant door, strode over to the table and sat opposite Finch.

"Hi there." His face bore an expression of enormous self-satisfaction.

"Hello." Now that he'd been forced away from talking about the slugs discovered in the bear's gut, Finch could barely acknowledge the intern.

"You know, the video technology we use is state-of-the-art." Bemused, Manfred grinned at Finch. "I had a chance to forward the necropsy video clip of your double-pirouette to my classmates at Oregon Health and Science. I think it's going to be a hit."

"What?"

"Yeah, the dean emailed me back to say it's already going viral on You Tube."

"Are you serious?" Finch's voice rose a notch. This was exactly the sort of thing that could destroy his credibility on the story. "Really?"

"No." Manfred nodded yes, but was saying, no. A smile stretched across his face.

"Which is it? Yes or no?"

Jennie laughed and put her coffee mug aside. "Lighten up, Finch. Just because we live in the backwoods doesn't mean we drink the local moonshine." She waved to the waitress and mouthed the words, "Check please."

When she saw the look of dread lingering in Will's face she added, *"It's a joke."*

"Sorry. Just kidding," Manfred said in an apologetic voice. "Had you there!"

Finch tried to laugh. "All right, let's move on."

CHAPTER SIX

DONNEL SMEARDON STOOD behind the shrubs bordering the cemetery on Miller Lane and waited for Sheriff Gruman to kill the squad car engine. The vehicle was standard issue, a Ford Crown Victoria Police Interceptor, black-and-white with a gold badge emblazoned on the front doors. When the engine switched off, Donnel could sense the world shrinking around him. That afternoon a thick fog had rolled in from the Pacific and he felt a chill crossing his shoulders. A shiver flushed through his spine.

The darkness and fog provided a screen and at this time of night he figured the chance of anyone spotting him as he climbed into Gruman's car was close to zero. He wished he still had the iPhone. Then he could secretly record the conversation he was about to have with the sheriff. His insurance policy. He'd recorded every word Gruman had spoken when he'd busted Donnel last weekend, and if the cop ever threatened him, he'd replay their conversation on CNN. Another Anderson Cooper scoop. It'd be enough to put Gruman away for a long time. He was sure of that. Certain of it. All the more reason to get the phone back from Ben Argyle.

He stepped onto the road and tapped on the passenger windshield. It lowered a few inches and he tipped his head toward the opening. When he couldn't make out anyone at the wheel he whispered in a shallow voice. "Sheriff?"

"Open the door and sit yourself inside."

Donnel pressed his lips together as he opened the door and sat on the passenger seat. He could smell tobacco, years of it oozing from the upholstery.

"Close the door, Donnel," Gruman said and pointed a thumb to the roof. "Even the ghosts can see you sitting here when the dome light's on."

He shut the door and settled in the chair. You're here now, he told himself. Best to keep this ride as short as possible.

"Good to see you, Donnel-o." Mark Gruman pulled a Lucky Strike from the pack in his pocket and fit it to his lips. He pushed in the dashboard lighter and squared his shoulders to the boy. "You asked, I answered. Now, tell me why I'm here."

"It's about the stuff you borrowed from me last weekend, Sheriff." Donnel stole a glance around the car. It appeared much the same as it looked last time he sat here, minutes after being busted by Gruman in the park outside Suomi Hall. He'd been forced to unload a dozen one-ounce baggies of marijuana from his backpack. And forced to surrender Ben Argyle's gun. His only victory, a small one, lay in the five baggies he'd hidden in his pants. Gruman hadn't demanded a strip search. At least he wasn't a pervert. That alone suggested to Donnel that he could possibly trust Gruman. Maybe.

"Borrowed?" The sheriff laughed at this and shook his

head with a look of surprise. He pressed the dash lighter to the tip of his cigarette. "Now what exactly do you think I *borrowed* from you? Certainly not that stash of hybrid marijuana that you illegally acquired from Jackie Spitzer."

Donnel's head dropped a notch toward his chest. "Did he talk to you?"

"Talk to me?" Gruman let out a grunt of disbelief. "Donnel, look at me." He waited until the boy's eyes swept past his face and then added, "I said, look at me." Donnel's eyes wobbled and then held. "Now tell me who I am."

He shrugged his shoulders and glanced away.

With his free hand Gruman reached across the car and turned Donnel's chin towards him. The gesture was gentle, almost tender. "Donnel, tell me, what am I?"

"You're…" he sputtered "…you're Astoria's sheriff."

Gruman released the boy's head and smiled. "Wrong. I'm Astoria's *fucking* sheriff." He drew on his cigarette. The ember glowed at the center of the darkness surrounding them. "You know, last fall I was re-elected for a fifth term in this county. Won by the biggest electoral margin in eighty-eight years. Not that anyone pays attention to details like that. But what's important about those numbers, Donnel, is the trust it conveys from the county to me. The respect the citizens have. The assurance that I will maintain our safety and security. That we can all sleep at night. That girls can walk unmolested. That we're free of pedophiles. *And drugs."* He paused, took another long drag on his Lucky. "And therefore it's incumbent upon me to talk to every thief, pimp and dope dealer from here to Tillamook. People like Jackie. People like *you."* He smiled again and felt the warmth of his power. He knew his reach was limited, but within his county — and certainly within this car — it was absolute. "So tell me, Donnel, what exactly is it that you think I *borrowed* from you."

Donnel moistened his lips. He felt his guts drop open, his heart thud in his throat. All sense of control began to slip from him. "The Glock," he said finally. "The nine-millimeter pistol. I need it back."

This was promising. Last time, Gruman couldn't squeeze any information about the semi-automatic pistol from the boy. He'd been too cocky, too sure that he had some inalienable rights that would shield him from divulging who owned the Glock. That was fine. Gruman knew the pistol was stolen and therefore valuable to someone. And he was certain that this nugget of information would slip into his hands sometime soon. Most likely within the next ten minutes. "Give it back? Then who would you give it back to?"

Donnel nodded unsteadily. "Can't say."

"Donnel. Look at me again." He took a final drag from his Lucky and squashed the butt in the ashtray. Once he had Donnel's attention he exhaled a dense cloud of smoke. "Now I want you to remember what I've done for you. Let's face the facts. You've already been booked, printed and sent to juvenile detention for two months. Just six months ago, am I right?" He paused to observe Donnel nod his head. "And just recently I relieved you of criminal possession of a narcotic substance. Enough, I might add, to make a criminal rap for intent to traffic." He held up a finger and then another. "Next, I relieved you of a stolen weapon." A third finger rose in the stale air.

"While it may still happen, so far I've reserved my decision to notify the local courts of *any* charges against you." A fourth finger now stood with the others. "And I am speaking civilly to you right now. Instead of cuffing you, I am saving your fucking brown ass from the jailhouse plaything it *will become* if I present you to a judge and jury. Now do you understand what I have done for you?"

Donnel squeezed his abdominal muscles and prayed that he would not shit. "Yes," he whispered.

"As you well know, I knew your father. We spent weeks fishing together." He shook his head dismissively. "I am trying to *save* you. Don't you get that?"

Donnel felt the world collapsing around him. His father dead. Mother gone to who-knows-where. "I know."

"All right, let's try one final time: Who owns the Glock?"

"Ben Argyle's dad." The words spilled out of him in one breath. He could barely believe the sense of relief flooding through him. It felt so powerful that he quickly added. "But I never used that gun. I only had it for show in case Jackie Spitzer put up a fight. I never fired it once."

Argyle? Gruman lifted a hand to his mouth and considered the possibilities. A trump card. Argyle, for Christ sakes.

"I swear I did not fire that gun at nobody, Sheriff." Donnel shuddered. A tear began to slip down his cheek.

Gruman felt a tinge of elation rise through his veins. He had so many options. With the journalist probing into things, now he could make a few bluffs. Throw some straw into the wind and let Will Finch fly after it. "All right. I believe you, Donnel. Still, there's a price you've got to pay."

D. F. Bailey

Donnel felt his chest tighten again. "A price?"

"Nothing to worry about." Gruman rested his fingers on the steering wheel. "You ever seen my boat out on the water?"

"The Gold Coaster?"

Gruman nodded.

"Yeah, I've seen it."

"I've got four prawn traps waiting for me just south of Clatsop Spit. I could use a hand pulling them up." As he smiled, his lips thinned and pulled tight over his yellow teeth. "Are you up for a two-hour run out in the salt chuck?"

※

The Gold Coaster was a lobster boat, a flat-decked working boat with the wheelhouse set in the bow and a retro-fitted diesel engine that enabled Gruman to cruise the Pacific coast for almost two days without refueling. Everyone in the office had laughed when they saw the "prize" that their sheriff had purchased at auction for six thousand dollars. Despite the sheriff's bluster and boast, to everyone else *The Gold Coaster* appeared to be a clunker. Built back in Maine, it was worn, old, noisy, awkward, slow. But a thorough inspection proved that it had been properly maintained. A back-to-the-grain paint job restored the finish, and with a new diesel engine Gruman knew the boat would swim like a fish. Besides, he'd learned a lot about lobster boats the one summer he spent in Bangor with his uncle aboard *The Skillet.* Together they'd ridden out the tail end of an early season hurricane that took down six other boats. "A lobster boat, Mark," Uncle Frank had told him as they pulled into the Bangor harbor. "You can't even push 'em under the water."

Gruman led their way onto the wharf and down the third finger to his boat. He pointed a narrow-beam LED flashlight straight ahead as he slipped quietly along the rubber deck pads. He'd instructed Donnel Smeardon to keep his mouth shut until the boat cleared the harbor. "In this fog," he'd told him, "sound carries right into the center of town."

The boat swayed and dipped as Donnel's feet left the wharf and landed on deck. "Never been on a boat before," he whispered. "I didn't think they wobbled so bad."

"Just set your feet wide apart and you'll steady out." Gruman tossed his satchel into the wheelhouse and started the ignition. While the engine began to warm he unknotted the ties from their stays and pulled all the lines aboard. Then he led Donnel into the wheelhouse, closed the door and pointed to the bench seat on the starboard. "Just sit there. Your work doesn't start until we reach the prawn traps. Depending on the tide, it could be an hour." He turned on the GPS and radar navigation screens and lit another Lucky Strike while he waited for the GPS to acquire its satellites. When they had a fix, he shut the overhead light, pushed the choke down to a low idle and listened to the engine's baritone hum. When everything was operational he lit a propane spot-heater and rubbed his hands above the corona of heat that it cast into the air.

"Everything ready?" Donnel's voice betrayed some doubt. He could see two or three boats on both sides of *The Gold Coaster*, but beyond that, everything slid into the mist. How could anyone navigate their way out of the harbor in this fog, let alone down river and out to Clatsop Spit?

"Just enjoy the ride, Donnel." He flicked on the night

lights, set the transmission in reverse and eased out of the slip. When he skirted the edge of the jetty, he pulled the wheel hard to the right, popped the engine into low gear and set them on a course to the entrance of the wharf, the engine whispering a bass melody now, pushing them forward a mere knot or two faster than the current.

After they'd cleared the marina, the boat eased into the slow westward flow of the Columbia River. At this point the current was modified by the tidal action of the Pacific, and now that the tide was ebbing, it dragged the boat forward at a good clip.

"Have you any idea why I've got you out here with me, Donnel?" Gruman asked as he glanced back at the bridge.

The boy turned toward Gruman, studied the green and blue shadows cast onto his face by the GPS and radar screens. "I thought it was for the prawns."

"Partly." He stood at the wheel and gazed into the mist ahead of the boat. "But it's also to give you a sense of living beyond the foster home you're in. Among other things." He frowned and thought about the care homes he'd seen over the years. "By the way, who's your foster mom?"

"Jill Hudson."

"Jill." He nodded. He'd known Jill from tenth grade. On grad night Scoop Bensen had knocked her up, then she disappeared for some years and suddenly materialized on the arm of Jeremy Stent, a fisherman who went missing in a storm five years ago. The Coast Guard dragged his swamped seiner into Astoria, all hands lost at sea. By then Jill had three more kids in tow and decided to use the foster program as a built-in meal-helper for her own brood. "Well, she'll keep you warm and fed," he said and looked to the boy.

Donnel shook his head and stared at the ship's clock on the wall. Five-twenty. He felt like he was back in juvie. Life was all about flopping from bed to sofa to dining hall chairs — and staring at the clock. And now this: slave labor for the local sheriff. He decided to wait out the rest of the night in silence, pull Gruman's fucking prawns on board and after that, see what what he could do to recover the Glock.

"And she's a looker," Gruman continued, with the image of Jill in mind. "You know, she's always had that bundle of red hair." When he saw Donnel look away he kicked up the throttle and pushed the boat toward the ocean. The fog seemed to be thinning and with luck, they'd discover it was just an onshore system that they'd clear when they passed the mouth of the river into the sea.

Gruman considered Donnel's silence as a form of defiance. Fine. So be it. Just makes the end-game that much easier to play. Still, obviously the boy had lessons to learn and Gruman was in a teaching mood.

"You know I've seen a lot of people go through this life without ever living it." He let this idea sit a moment and then continued. "People doing jobs they hate, marrying women they soon can't abide, raising their kids like strangers. When they see it in themselves, this disaffection, it can become a drowning pool. They start numbing themselves with booze and drugs. Internet porn. Just one long sequence of mindless diversions." He looked at Donnel. "You know what I mean?"

Donnel flexed his shoulders. He decided it might be

smarter to play along. "Yeah. I've seen it."

Gruman nodded. "Maybe in your own family. Maybe in yourself, right?"

"What the fuck?" Donnel shot him a look of despair. "I don't know, man. Shit, I'm just trying to get by."

"I know." He felt a small spark of sympathy and quickly snuffed it out. "You know the years I spent in the military, they marked the beginning of my life. Desert Storm. The concentration of awareness you acquire. The intensity of life flowing second by second in your veins. That moment when the man next to you disappears in a vapor of blood mist." He paused and cocked his head. "Oh yeah, I've seen it. And *lived it.*"

Donnel held a hand over his mouth. For a moment he thought Gruman had lost his mind. "How long until we get to the prawn traps?"

Gruman shrugged. " 'nother ten minutes."

"Then what do we do?"

"I got four buoys. We pull them up one at a time, empty the prawn traps into the catch bin, re-bait them, slip them overboard. Job done."

"Then we head back, right?"

Gruman considered this. He didn't want to lie to the boy. He wanted to face this with honesty, not deception. "Soon as we're done, I'll be turning *The Gold Coaster* straight back to Astoria. Just in time for breakfast."

When they passed the tip of Clatsop Spit the coastal current pulled the bow to port. Gruman turned the wheel and within five minutes he spotted the first buoy. His were painted with red and yellow stripes and he'd tied each one to a six-inch flag that caught the light offshore breeze. The fog had completely dissipated now and in the moonlight the visibility was excellent. He cut the engine to an idle and set the transmission in neutral.

"I can't believe how bright it is out here," Donnel said as he followed Gruman onto the deck.

"Don't talk, Donnel." He sucked in a lungful of air. "Just feel it. Can you feel it?"

"You mean like the air. And the way the boat rolls on the waves."

He nodded. The boy had it now. The feeling of the universe pouring into your body.

He made his way to the side of the boat, pulled the electric pull-reel from the hold and mounted it onto the gunwale and locked it in place. "See that gaff strapped to the deck over there? Grab it and stand beside me."

Donnel raised the pole above his head. It was at least ten feet long. One end was fitted with a six-inch brass spike that curled into a three-quarter turn, perfectly designed to snag a tow line from the water. When he mastered the balance, he walked over to Gruman and set the mid-point of the gaff on the gunwale.

"Now look. I'm going to bring the boat alongside the buoy. As we pass, set the gaff into the water, then catch the line under the buoy with the gaff and draw it on board." He looked him in the eyes. "Got it?"

Donnel tested the heft of the gaff in his hands and nodded. "Bring the buoy right on board?"

"Exactly. All right. You're on your own." Don't fall in, he

97

almost added, but thought better of it as he walked back into the wheelhouse.

Donnel felt *The Gold Coaster* shift as it slipped back into gear and the engine nudged the boat forward. He set his feet and re-established his balance, then dipped the gaff into the water as they neared the first buoy. When he saw the line just below the belly of the buoy he angled the gaff under the line, felt it pull tight and lifted it into the air. The heaviness dragged through his hands. He pulled the line tight and when the buoy hit the gunwale, he snagged it with his left hand. For a moment he felt the gaff slip from his right hand but secured it before it fell into the sea. "Got it!" he called. An exhilaration filled him and he turned to the wheelhouse and smiled at Gruman.

Gruman glanced at him from the cabin, disengaged the transmission, and cut back the throttle. By the time he made it back to the pull-reel, Donnel had set the gaff on the deck and secured the buoy and the line that ran from it over the gunwale and down to the prawn trap on the seabed.

"Give me the line," Gruman said and coiled a length of the cord around the circumference of the first wheel of the pull-reel. Two grooved wheels, like the reels at the ends of a clothesline, were shackled together on a steel frame, one on top of the other. He adjusted the prawn line around the twelve-inch wheel and then fed it onto the smaller six-inch reel. Once the power was engaged, the pull-reel could haul a hundred-pound catch onto the boat within five minutes. He fiddled with the wiring and in a moment he had the system up and running. It turned through two rotations and Gruman sat at a stool beside it, feeding the wet cable into a circular coil on the deck as the line came off the second wheel.

"When you see the prawn trap break the surface, lean over and haul it onto the deck. Understand?"

"Got it." Donnel gazed into the water, mesmerized by the rope pulling strands of slimy green seaweed into the boat. "Look at that."

Gruman nodded. The kid was getting it. He could say with certainty that Donnel had tasted a little of reality. That the boy's life wouldn't be completely wasted.

"There it is!" Donnel anchored his feet to the deck when the prawn trap broke the surface. "I got it." He leaned over and hauled the circular aluminum frame onto the lip of the gunwale. He shook the trap and a small eel slithered out of the netting into the ocean. "Man, it's full!" With a second heave he dumped it onto the deck. He leaned over to inspect a copper tag attached to the frame. It took a moment for him to piece together the series of letters stamped onto the tag. *Mark Gruman.*

Gruman clicked off the power supply to the pull-reel and examined the catch. At least a hundred prawns squirmed in the net, their spiky hairs twitching madly from their pink shells. On average they looked to be two to three inches in length, and fat as his thumbs. A good catch, especially if the three remaining traps held this bounty. He lifted the trap onto the stern platform and showed Donnel how to empty the mesh into the the big plastic hold, remove the collateral catch — a small octopus and a dogfish — rinse the prawns down, re-bait the bait tub, close the netting with the two bungee cords and cast it back into the sea.

※

99

Donnel was fascinated by the whole operation. Over the next hour they retrieved the second and third traps. Now he stared at the fourth buoy in the distance. They were back in the wheelhouse, trying to warm their backs against the propane heater under the clock. "Anyone ever steal your catch?"

"Hard to tell. Sometimes I've hauled up an empty trap or two." He shrugged to suggest it was not common. "On the whole, I think fishermen respect one another. Not like people you find elsewhere," he added. Better not to belabor the point, he decided. Especially now that they were down to the last twenty minutes or so. "Okay, let's snag this last buoy, and then we're done. But first, I've got something for you."

Donnel turned from the window to look at the sheriff. "What?"

"What you were asking for." He reached into his satchel and drew the Glock into his hand.

Donnel stared at the gun. It was wrapped in a sealed plastic bag, the sort of thing you'd see on a cop show, he thought, to ensure the fingerprints weren't messed up. Funny, since he'd stepped on the boat, he hadn't considered it. Part of him hated the gun. Another part was obsessed by it.

"You paid your dues." Gruman opened the seal so that the handle faced the boy. "Take it."

Donnel lifted the pistol in his hand. His again. And he belonged to it. Ben Argyle could keep the iPhone; this is what he wanted. He set his teeth and aimed the gun at the fourth buoy, then tucked the pistol under his belt at the back of his jeans and zipped his jacket so the Glock was secure.

"That would count as concealing a weapon." Gruman

looked at him and smiled at this little joke.

"Not if *you* know where it is," Donnel shot back.

Gruman tipped his head and frowned. The kid's old attitude back with a vengeance. There'd be no reforming Donnel Smeardon, he knew that much. Best to nip this thorn at the stem.

"Let's get this last float up," he said and cut the throttle and turned the wheel so that the starboard side of the boat would glide past the buoy.

Donnel stepped onto the deck and closed the wheelhouse door. He felt the tension of the gun against his spine. What could stop him from taking out Gruman right now? He'd have his gun and be free and clear of any more intimidation. Of course, he didn't know how to run *The Gold Coaster,* so until they made it back to the harbor, he'd be at the mercy of the currents and tides. Best to wait. Bide some time. Besides, likely the old man was packing his own heat.

He put these thoughts aside and dipped the gaff under the line and pulled the cable over the gunwale. "Got it," he called to Gruman, and then lifted the float onto the deck.

Gruman cut the engine and set up the pull-reel again and began to furl the trap line onto the deck. "You're starting to get the swing of that thing. Too bad."

Donnel gazed into the slate-gray water, eager to spot the rising trap before it broke the surface. "Why *too bad?*"

"It's a shame to see a man with a useful skill fail to use it."

Donnel bit into his lower lip. He could barely contain the fury rising through his chest. Gruman had completely lost it now. Who even knew what the fuck he was talking about?

"You ever had a woman, Donnel?"

"What?"

"Sex. With a woman."

"Course I have." He turned his back and yelled, *"Fuck!"*

"Just wondering. Just wanted to be sure of that." He glanced over the gunwale. The rising trap was now visible. "Have an eye. Thar she blows."

Donnel grabbed the frame and hauled the trap on board. Like the previous three traps, it shuddered with hundreds of plump, writhing prawns. He lifted it over the gunwale, then set it on the stern and began to release the prawns into the plastic hold. All told, they must have over six hundred prawns. He couldn't figure how much money that might draw in. Maybe six hundred dollars?

"Okay, rinse that out and reset the bait. But don't toss it overboard until I tell you." As he stood next to the pull-reel, Gruman studied the boy's lean back and shoulders as he worked. He lit a Lucky and took a long easy drag on it. "And pass me the gaff, would you?"

"What am I — your slave?" Donnel knelt down, picked up the gaff and passed it to Gruman. Then he turned his attention to the trap, baited it and closed the netting with two bungee cords.

The sheriff snugged the end of the gaff under his armpit and continued. "Since this is the last trap, I want to unhitch the reeler before we let her go. So wrap the line around your wrist four or five turns before you cast it off. Just to secure it."

Donnel pulled the nylon rope tight above his wrist. "Like this?"

Gruman glanced at the line. "Yeah."

"Just tell me when you want me to toss the trap in." He turned to the sheriff and watched him disassemble the pull-reel and wait for his signal. It would be the last time he would see Gruman.

"Okay. Throw it over."

He braced his knees on the gunwale and heaved the trap back into the ocean. At the same moment, Gruman pressed the curled brass tip of the gaff into the middle of Donnel's back, at a point a few inches above the bulge formed by the Glock pistol. With one deft jab he shoved the boy overboard and into the water. In his panic Donnel grasped for anything that came to hand. He tugged wildly on the nylon rope. With the trap line wrapped over his forearm he imagined that he might be saved, that Gruman would grab the unfurling cable and haul him to the surface. But in his last, frantic seconds he realized that the line was secured only to the sinking prawn trap. As the trap dragged him down to the seabed his lungs expelled his last breath in an explosion of tiny, almost invisible bubbles that dissipated into the gray abyss.

Gruman flicked his cigarette over the side and gazed into the open ocean below the boat. He checked his watch and forced himself to wait five minutes before he moved. When Donnel failed to reappear, he dipped the gaff under the buoy, pulled it onto the deck, cut the cable with a fillet knife and let the line slip into the sea. He set the orphaned buoy next to the prawn catch and shook his head.

An hour later he made a point of tracking down Toby Pearson, the wharf manager, and lured him alongside *The Gold*

Coaster.

"Somebody stole one of my traps," he said to Pearson with a look of disbelief on his face. He held the two-foot length of rope in his hand, one end still attached to the buoy, and fingered the edge where it had been cut. "You can see where they sheared it off. Clean cut, like from a filleting knife," he added. "No accident, that. Work of a damned poacher, I'd say."

CHAPTER SEVEN

WILL FINCH STOPPED the Ford Tempo at the side of the gravel road and studied the surrounding landscape. This must be it, he told himself, the exact spot where Toeplitz had parked his Mercedes. He stepped out of the car, slung his courier bag over his shoulder and stood a moment to listen to the overwhelming silence. Even in the faint amber glow of the mid-afternoon, the ridge seemed bleaker than when he'd driven up the switchback with Ben Argyle. A light wind swept up the desolate slope and a shiver ran down his spine. He zipped his jacket to his throat and tugged his cap onto his head.

With an even, measured step he paced the distance to the spot where Toeplitz's remains had been found. Sixty-five steps. Then he stood on the edge of the wide hill where the bear had escaped and disappeared. Somewhere down there the beast had hidden away for several days. A good place to conceal almost anything.

He dug through his courier bag and withdrew the ziploc baggie where he'd stored the two brass shell casings from the Argyles' rifles. He took one of the brass into his hand and swept the ground for a stone of the same size. He tested the heft of two or three rocks against the weight of the brass and when he found a good match, he drew an X across the face of the rock with a yellow highlighter pen. Then he placed the brass back in the ziploc and dropped it into his bag.

Directly below him he spotted a break in the trees and scrub. He swung his arm back and forth, thinking of his days in Little League baseball and the tight pitches he could fire across home plate when he was fourteen. After a crisp wind-up, he threw the rock toward the break. He watched it disappear into the weeds and then heard the sharp knock as it tagged a tree stump. Maybe fifty feet. The arm's not quite as good as it once was, he conceded.

As he walked down the hill toward the break, he assessed the landscape more closely. The bank dropped at a ten-degree angle, he figured. Dozens of scrub trees, mostly alders, were just beginning to green. Compared to the lush forests on the coast, the alpine vegetation seemed delayed by a month, maybe two. Only the grass was in full bloom and it waved in the breeze, the green buds slapping at his thighs as he pushed forward.

When he reached the clearing he stood a moment, his eyes sweeping the ground for the small rock. Nothing. Then he spotted a broken sapling that had been snapped in two leaving a three-inch stump still rooted in the ground. Perhaps in his fury the bear had crashed against the young alder on his flight down the hill.

Again, his eyes raked the ground and *there* — about two feet to his left — lay the rock with the yellow X painted on its face.

"So from here," he said, lifting his left arm in a line parallel to the gravel road above, "is where we might find ... something." He marked a half-dead cedar in the distance. If he made it to that old tree without finding anything of value, then he'd give up the search.

He spotted an inch-thick stick on the ground and broke away the small stems and loose bark that still clung to the wood. With one, two, three passes of the stick he swept the grass around him and began to step toward the distant cedar tree, walking parallel to the switchback and adjusting his distance from the road to match the fifty feet he'd thrown the rock. He moved in half steps, slowing to ensure that he cleared the grasses underfoot before he took a new step forward. After thirty minutes, he reached another clearing and there his eye caught a glint of light.

"Wouldn't you know." He kneeled next to the brass cylinder, marveling at his luck. He drew his cellphone from his bag and took several pictures of the bullet casing where it lay. He tugged on his latex gloves, then lifted the brass into his palm. "Hmm," he whispered aloud. "What have we here?"

Finch sealed the shell casing in a second ziploc and continued his search. Ten feet along he found the second piece of brass. He took three more still pictures, then stood up and captured a three-hundred-sixty degree sweep of the entire ridge with his video camera. Then he stored the second bullet shell in the ziploc, nestled it in his courier bag and plodded directly up the hill in a perpendicular line to the road.

When he reached the gravel track he looked back toward his car to determine where he stood in relation to Toeplitz's body and his abandoned Mercedes. "Maybe half a mile," he whispered and tugged his jacket collar over his neck. The wind kicked at the grass and tree limbs. Time to head back.

He set his bag on the ground, took another picture of where it lay and then walked back to the Ford Tempo. As he turned the car around he set the trip meter on the odometer to zero. When he retrieved his bag from the side of the road, the trip-meter read zero-point-six miles.

"So, Sherlock," he said as the car began the long descent down Saddle Mountain, "after the shooter pumped two nine-millimeter bullets into Raymond Toeplitz, he collected the brass from the crime scene. Then a little over half a mile into his escape, he stopped, got out of his car and tossed the evidence into the scrub. Smart. But not quite smart enough."

※

Will glanced around the Three Cups Coffee House and wondered how to convince Jennie Lee to confide in him again. Just dive in, he told himself. This woman isn't receptive to nuance and subtlety.

"Look. I'm going to show you something. And if what I have to show you has any relation to the bullets I saw you and Manfred extract from the guts of that bear, I simply want you to acknowledge it. Okay?"

She paused to scratch her head. A distraction. "All right."

Finch lifted the leather flap on his courier bag and pulled out the ziploc he'd used to store the nine-millimeter brass that he'd found up on the switchback.

Her eyes narrowed as she studied the bullet casings. "And those are what, exactly?"

"Nine-mille brass," he said. "And my bet is they will match the slugs you found in the bear."

"Where did you get them?"

"Just below Lookout Point on Saddle Mountain where Raymond Toeplitz was murdered." He clicked the photo gallery icon on his phone and swept through several images until he reached the sequence of pictures he'd taken on the mountain.

Jennie studied the photographs in silence and returned the phone to Will. She set her eyes on the Columbia River as it slipped under the bridge toward the Pacific Ocean. After another moment she said, "All right, it looks legitimate. But what does it get us?"

Will's face flushed with surprise. He laughed, an incredulous gasp. "Are you serious?" He shook the ziploc just enough to make the brass ring together. "I'm literally holding half the puzzle in my hand. You've got the other half back in your office. If they match, it will tell us something."

"Tell us what, precisely?"

A look of frustration crossed his face. She was playing devil's advocate. Now he'd have to spell out the details.

"That Raymond Toeplitz was shot and left for dead in his SUV. The shooter threw the physical evidence — these brass casings — into the bush six-tenths of a mile from the scene of the crime. The bear then dragged Toeplitz from his car and began to devour him. As part of his meal" — Finch grimaced at the thought — "he consumed the two slugs which killed Toeplitz, the same bullets you extracted from the bear. Toeplitz wasn't killed by the bear. He was murdered before the bear found him."

She nodded as if she were considering two or three other possibilities. "Okay. Are there any fingerprints on them?"

"I don't know. Probably just partials. To be sure, we need to get them to a lab."

As Jennie hesitated again, Will realized he needed to be more persuasive. Without her half of the puzzle, his evidence alone didn't warrant a homicide investigation.

"Jennie, step back a minute to consider what we've put together. If your forensics team can match these two pieces of brass to the two slugs you extracted from the bear, you'll possess enough street cred to seize Toeplitz's car *and* request a formal inquest into his death. You won't need Sheriff Gruman's permission. You won't need anything else."

She pressed her lips together and nodded.

"But first" — he held a finger in the air — "first, I want you to guarantee me that we keep our deal."

She narrowed her eyes and considered this. "Okay." Finally she seemed able to muster the determination needed to press forward. "The deal is still on. Let's see if the brass match the bullets we found in the bear."

"All right." He smiled, certain now that the case would break wide open.

"But if they do, Will, I hope you realize that we're into a whole new level of trouble."

※

When they returned to the pit, Will immediately saw that the room had been transformed since his ignominious exit.

After he'd extracted brain tissues from the bear to check for rabies or other neurological disease, Manfred had incinerated the corpse and restored the work space to a state of professional hygiene and order. All that remained of the bear were the audio and video recordings of the necropsy — and their collective memory of it.

Once again the three of them relived Finch's fainting episode, and after another round of laughter he steered the conversation to the business at hand. Jennie told Manfred about the new puzzle concerning the bullets and brass casings and said that they needed to examine them in the lab. She led the way down a windowless corridor. Manfred followed her and Finch brought up the rear.

He pulled the ziploc from his bag, opened it and carefully slid the brass onto the stainless steel bench next to Jennie. "I haven't touched these with anything organic," he said. "Just so we could dust them for prints."

"This is only a preliminary examination, by the way," she said as she lifted the metal casings on the tip of a needle. "ME's don't handle weapons forensics, so whatever we discover has to be sent to the forensics lab for verification."

Finch nodded. From years of reporting he understood the distinctions.

"But still, we can make some informed guesses. First, let's see if they're the same caliber and check for any obvious similarities." She tugged on her gloves and then clicked on an overhead lamp and placed the two slugs and shells side-by-side on a black cloth. Despite the warping the bullets endured, they appeared to make a superficial match to the brass. "Looks like the bullets and casings are both nine-millimeter," she said.

"Agreed." Manfred took a flash photograph and tilted his head to one side to consider what the match might mean. "But these bullets weren't *shot* at the bear. After a second evaluation I couldn't find any entry wounds in the bear carcass that would correspond to nine-millimeter slugs." He paused and took a step away from the examination table. "Oh my God…. He *ate* them."

Finch smiled. Look who's just arrived at the game. Better late than never.

"Exactly what I've been thinking," Jennie said. "And when Will showed me these bullet casings, it conferred more certainty. What it means? That I don't know." She moved to the far end of the bench and with a stainless steel tweezer she set one slug under a microscope, then peered through the lens and adjusted the focus and light mechanisms. Then she lay one of the casings below the scope and turned the brass slightly. "There, have a look. You can see micro alignments — tiny mechanical and manufacturing signatures — between the brass and the slug. And yes, *here* — that might be a trace of a fingerprint."

Finch examined the slug and shell through the lens. As a result of the impact, the slug had been transformed into a mushroom-shape after it hit its target. Once his eyes adjusted to the amplification, he could clearly see tiny dents at the edges of the brass and the base of the slug that seemed to carry from one to the other.

Jennie laid out the other pair and pressed her eyes to the scope. "This match is even more pronounced."

Manfred gazed through the lens. "Yeah. And has a better

fingerprint."

"Do you think they can lift it?"

"In the forensic lab?" He drew his head away from the microscope and he pressed his lips together. "Maybe."

"All right. Send them in for a complete diagnostic on all four pieces." She checked the wall clock: 2:33. "And we want to know the results on the bear's brain tissues. If you can have a report to me on everything by this time tomorrow, I'd appreciate it."

"What about the Wallenby file?"

"Move it back a day," she said and pulled the latex gloves from her hands. "And Manfred — if you happen to see Gruman, he doesn't need to know about any of this yet, okay?"

Manfred smiled with the same grin that had graced his face when he'd spooked Finch about posting the video of his faint on YouTube. He nodded and clicked off the microscope lamp.

Finch decided that he disliked the varnished look painted on the intern's mug. An expression of pleasure masking a sadistic humor. Sadly, it suited him.

CHAPTER EIGHT

BRENDA WHEELER LED Finch past the floor-to-ceiling windows to a table at the far end of the Bridgewater Bistro. "No fog, tonight," she said with a nod to the clear sky.

Finch studied the river as it flowed under the massive bridge. "It's gorgeous," he said and his eyes lingered on a pair of gulls coursing above the water. To his relief, they provided a respite of sorts, a break from another long day.

She smiled, passed him a menu, and advised him that his waitress would be along in a moment. Back at the hostess desk, she called Gianna Whitelaw, who was just finishing a latté at Three Cups Coffee House, a few blocks down the road. Gianna had heard from Brenda's sister, Jill Sutton, that Finch had visited Three Cups on four occasions now. Jill knew these things because she worked in the sheriff's office and Gruman had directed everyone to keep an eye on the reporter from San Francisco. Gianna smiled. One way or the other she knew that she'd bump into Finch that evening, she just didn't know if their meeting would be by accident or by design.

Like all of the Whitelaws, Gianna had spent a year living in Clatsop County. Her great-grandfather established the tradition a few years after he built the lodge. The idea was to ensure his children appreciated the natural lifestyle and the people who lived and worked in small towns surrounded by "unsullied wilderness" as he called it. Even if it meant withdrawing his offspring from their preparatory schools and sports academies for two or three years at a time, the old man insisted on the change of pace. And his children, grandchildren and great-grandchildren all loved it. They referred to the year-long residency as doing a "rotation," as if they could roll out of the programmed pace of their urban lives and find an inner sense of purpose in the family lodge. One by one, rotation by rotation, each of the Whitelaws built friendships and laid down their individual roots in the community.

During her rotation Gianna met Brenda and Jill, and all of their friends in Astoria and Cannon Beach. Gianna's twin half-brothers and her two half-sisters had done the same. Her father, too, spent a year on rotation and actually attended Astoria High School in the 1960s. That's where Senator Franklin Whitelaw met Mark Gruman's oldest brother. Over the decades Mark, now the county sheriff, became a family confidante — a friend who'd spared Gianna from DUI charges on more than one occasion.

※

Gianna Whitelaw eased her Mercedes-Benz C320 Sport Coupe into the Bridgewater Bistro parking lot and glanced at Will Finch's Ford Tempo. She cut the ignition and thought a moment about her plans. Then she drew down the sun visor mirror and primped her hair. No lipstick smudges, no runny eyeliner. Not bad for a bereaved girlfriend.

At the desk she met Brenda Wheeler, who tipped her head toward Finch's table.

"Thanks," Gianna whispered and made her way to the bar where the bartender fixed her a Margarita.

She took a sip and walked to the far end of the room. As she approached Finch she fixed her face with a look of dawning surprise. "Oh," she said when she drew beside him. "It's Mr. Finch."

Finch shifted his eyes away from his cell phone. He'd been studying the photos he'd taken of Toeplitz's car. "Hi. What are you doing here?"

She scanned the room as if she were looking for spies. "Had to get away from the family. The hostess is an old friend so I thought I'd pop in."

"Pop in," Finch mimed her tone and put his phone away. "Please, have a seat." He pointed to the chair opposite and considered the probability that she might stumble into him here. Small town, after all.

As she settled into the chair he studied her. He could tell she'd had a drink or two, but she seemed able to hold them. She was still dressed in black, but now attired in a sleeveless cocktail dress with a discrete scoop neck that hinted at the volume of her breasts. Tasteful, he thought. For a woman in mourning.

"Have you eaten?"

"No, but — "

"I insist," he said and passed the menu to her. "Your timing's perfect. I just decided what I want but the waitress hasn't come by."

Finch ordered poisson St. Jacques and a bottle of Perrier, Gianna the Caesar salad with a side of prawns and a second Margarita.

"No booze for you?" She tilted her head to one side, a gesture to determine if he felt ill.

"No, not tonight."

"Really?" Another look of surprise crossed her face. "From my vantage point, which is already two sheets to the wind, you look stone sober."

He laughed. "I just climbed onto the wagon about a month ago. Trying to see if I can stay on it for another few weeks."

"Oh." She looked away with an air of confusion. "Well, then," she hesitated, "maybe I shouldn't — "

"No, please." He sensed her awkwardness and for the first time since he'd departed Eden Veil he felt the burden of his sobriety. "Drink whatever you want, it's not an issue."

Finch decided to shift direction and steer the conversation to where they'd left off in the lodge kitchen when the senator had interrupted them. "Look, sorry I made such a bad impression on your father."

She pulled a cord of dark hair past her right shoulder and waved a hand to dismiss the idea. Her face took on a tinge of bitterness. "Believe me, unless your wallet is full of cash, no one can make a good first impression on Franklin."

"And I didn't realize how hard it hit you."

She glanced away again. Finch could see that she'd been hurt by Toeplitz's death. It wasn't mere affectation. He had to tread carefully.

"You mean Ray. I can't really talk about him yet. It's too

soon."

"Ray," he repeated. Finch leaned back in his chair and tried to take her measure. Her ribbons of hair, the distant look in her face, her obvious pedigree. She was born and raised in a world of enormous privilege. Overall she filled the room with a striking, even glamorous presence. Yet part of her inhabited a self-absorbed bubble.

"You know, I think I'm the one most surprised by how I feel." She frowned as if she wished she'd understood the power of Toeplitz's affections before he died. "You saw my family at the house today. It's all party games. Christ. It's been less than a week since...."

Finch sensed her discomfort and shifted his head to observe a freighter easing out toward the ocean. After a moment he turned his attention back to Gianna. "Look, maybe I shouldn't have — "

"No, no. You're the only person who actually knew him that I can talk to up here. None of *them* will talk about him." She leaned forward and held him with her eyes. "Because of the so-called betrayal."

Finch nodded. "You mean the trial? That he was going to testify for the District Attorney about the bitcoin fraud."

"That's all that mattered to Franklin and his brother. And the twins." Her mouth turned in disgust.

He wondered if he should disclose exactly how much he knew about Toeplitz and his situation with Whitelaw, Whitelaw & Joss. Did she understand that Toeplitz was about to smash their empire? He hesitated. Awkward as it was, now seemed like the right time to ask her to go on the record. "Gianna, it seems like a terrible time for this, but can I ask you some questions about the story I'm working on for the *eXpress?* For the record, I mean."

Her jaw tightened as she considered the options. She didn't expect to be talking so intimately about Ray and her family. On the other hand, she realized this was precisely why she'd tracked Finch down. She knew she was at a crossroads, but she couldn't make out what lay ahead. "All right."

Finch picked up his phone, scrolled to the recording app, pressed RECORD and set the phone on the table between them. He narrowed his eyes and smiled. "Okay. So we're on the record now, Gianna. I'm just going to add the date, time and place. For the record." In a neutral voice he spoke the necessary facts in the direction of the phone, then smiled at her.

"You were saying that Ray Toeplitz's testimony in the trial was all that mattered to your father and brothers. But what was it that mattered to you, Gianna?"

"I don't know *what* exactly. Like the other girls, we never were allowed to get that close to the company board room. Only Justin and Evan were admitted to the inner circle. But what mattered to me was the way they all cut him off."

"From?" He gave her a searching look.

"From his career at the firm. *He gave them ten years of his life.* And the firm was the only world he knew. No wife, no kids. No family." She shrugged at the final emptiness of Toeplitz's existence. "I imagine his will gives everything to some charity. Probably ASP."

"ASP?"

"Asperger's Support Programs." Her eyes narrowed as she

looked at him.

"Right." He nodded, glanced away and then smiled. "A friend of mine in journalism school had Asperger's. He was so shy. In the end he simply couldn't do the job. Not journalism anyway. He became a researcher instead. I still call him whenever I need information I can't dig up on my own."

"With Ray it was all numbers. Perfect for a finance mathematician, right? Except in the last six months. I think I actually opened a door for him."

"A door?" Finch realized that the interview had entered a predictable phase. Gianna had forgotten the recorder on the table, forgotten that she was on record. He also realized that an interview with Gianna required a series of probing questions to decode the meanings that lay beneath most of what she said. Despite her superficial looks and charms, she lived her life three or four layers below that surface.

She studied the puzzled look on his face. "Look, okay … he had Asperger's. But he was genius with numbers. Financial engineering. Everyone who worked with him knew it. Ask my Uncle Dean. No wait, *don't even talk to Dean!* The man is a sociopath." Her face displayed a bleak smile. She shrugged and continued.

"But despite the way Ray could hide it with strangers, he had no clue with people. At first, like most everybody who'd spent a few hours with him, I had this kind of pity for him. For his isolation. Then one day we were alone, sitting right here as it happens" — she directed a manicured finger at the table surface — "and he completely opened up to me. How he had these *feelings.* How he was so afraid of them. And then, wouldn't you know it, I took him on as project." She pressed her lips together and glanced away as if telling it aloud now and hearing it for the first time, she couldn't believe what she was saying. "And not just as a sympathy fuck, either. Turns out, he was a beautiful man. *Inside.*" She held up the index and middle fingers of her right hand and pressed them to her heart.

For a moment Finch couldn't think how to respond. In a whisper, he let out one word. "Wow."

Gianna tipped her head back and grinned, amused that she'd stymied him. She finished her drink and set it aside, then glanced around the room searching out the waitress. "Good. Here comes dinner. And my next drink."

As they began to eat, Finch realized that while Gianna might not know how her father had enticed Toeplitz for his final visit to the lodge, she could reveal the circumstances of his final departure. First, he needed some background details.

"So when did Toeplitz arrive? On Friday?"

She considered this a moment. "Yes. Just after we had dinner."

"And he stayed the night?"

"Yes, but in the guest room. He'd been up for hours, arguing with Franklin, or rather listening to Franklin blast him. Ray didn't *argue* about anything. Ever."

"And what happened the following day?

"Just like I told you. The last time Franklin and I saw him was in the kitchen. The situation was so tense, he couldn't even kiss me goodbye."

Finch nodded. Obviously she hadn't felt the need to hide her relationship with Toeplitz from the senator.

"Look, this is a personal question and you don't need to answer it, but how long had you and Ray been together?"

"You mean *joined at the hip?*" A wry look crossed her face. "That's the expression that Franklin used after he discovered our affair. About three months. Just long enough to make it count for something," she said as if little in her life counted for anything before her intimacy with Toeplitz.

Finch thought about the implications as he ate another piece of seafood. Then he remembered the exact words she'd used in the afternoon to describe Toeplitz's departure. He leaned forward and spoke to her in a clear, precise tone. "Gianna, you also said that your brothers *drove him out of there.* Do you mean they got into his car with him?"

"One of them did. Evan, I think. And Justin followed in his own car. Why?" She shrugged, wondered how this could be relevant.

"It's just for the record. I always try to get all the facts, so I can understand the context of the stories I write."

"Of course." She ate a prawn, chewed at it and then saw Finch's cellphone. "I forget that you're a reporter. Franklin hates that, by the way." She laughed. "Maybe that's why I'm telling you all this."

"That's up to you. Don't tell me anything you want left off the record."

"Fuck it," she said and waved a hand. "Ask me anything. If I don't want to answer, I won't."

"If there was so much tension before he left, why did Ray let Evan into the car with him?"

"Yeah. *That* was ridiculous." She took another sip of her

Margarita. "Ever since he'd come up here, since 2006 or 07, he always said he wanted to hike up to Saddle Mountain. It's off route 26 on the way into Portland. They gave him this big story about how they'd been promising to take him up there, and now you know, *better late than never*."

"That seems so … *staged*."

"Yeah, but that's part of Asperger's. Inability to decode social situations." She waved a hand again, this time in a short, angry chop. "When I saw what was happening I was so pissed at Franklin and my brothers. And when I realized Ray couldn't even hug me goodbye, I just left the room."

"And that was … the last time."

Gianna gazed through the window at the river. A tear slipped from her eye and she brushed it away.

Finch thought about his own world, the world in which he *didn't* grab Buddy from Bethany and refuse to let her drive him to the baseball game. "You know," he said after a moment, "it would be a mistake to blame yourself for this."

Her face tightened and another tear escaped from her eyes, then two more. She dabbed them away with her thumbs.

"That would be magical thinking," he continued. "When you think you can control people's fate." He'd learned the hard way what a self-destructive lie that was, the delusion that you can control someone else. "It's difficult just to manage yourself, don't you think?"

She nodded at the obvious. She could barely suppress her tears.

Despite the tension, Finch realized that he had to press on. "So Ray got into his car with Evan and Justin followed them."

She waited until she could take an even breath. "Yes."

"You saw them? What time was it?"

"From my bedroom window as they drove off. Around noon."

"And they got back, when?"

"About 10:30 that night. I was lying on my bed, awake, planning how I'd make it all up to Ray, realizing I had to make a break from my family. I had to choose between Ray and the Whitelaws. Then I heard Justin's car drive up the gravel road to the garage."

"Did you get up to see who it was?"

"No, but I heard them talking as they walked toward the house after the garage door went down."

"Could you hear what they said?"

"No. They were talking over one another. Not in an argument, but serious."

"You're sure it was them?"

She snarled in disgust. "I've been listening to my half-brothers since they were babies. Yeah, it was them." She finished off her Margarita and glanced around the room. Brenda walked past and they smiled to one another.

Finch wondered if she had more to reveal. "And then?"

She shrugged, picked at her salad and then set her fork aside. "And then the next day we heard the news. And ... about the bear." She looked at Finch and spotted his cellphone again. "Can you turn that off now?"

"Of course." He tapped the STOP button and slipped the phone into his pocket.

"So we're *off the record?*"

Finch heard a commotion at the front desk and turned to see what was happening. Four or five staff walked to the front window and peered at the marina. Two of them were pointing toward the waterfront. He couldn't make out anything unusual.

"Yes. Everything's off the record now." He smiled.

"Good. Because I have something else to confess." Her tongue slid back and forth between her lips. "Can I have a sip of your Perrier?"

"Sure." Pleased to see that she was shifting gears, he filled an empty wine glass with some water and passed it to her.

"I'm not really an alcoholic. Not a serious one, at least."

He shrugged, a gesture to let her know that her habits were none of his business.

"I think I just needed a few drinks to stiffen my nerve."

"Your nerve?"

She glanced away. "Okay. So ... I didn't *just* bump into you here."

"No?" A look of surprise crossed his face.

"Oh right. As if you didn't know it too." She shook her head with an expression that revealed they were both in on the game.

"Well, I wondered."

"You were easy to find, you know."

"Really." A statement, not a question.

"Uh-huh. Brenda's sister works in the sheriff's office." She raised her eyebrows. "Gruman's been keeping an eye on you."

"Are you serious?" Finch felt his stomach tighten. He didn't suspect he was on anyone's radar. "Why would he do that?"

"That's just Gruman." She frowned. "He's a control freak. The exact opposite of your theory. He thinks he can control *everybody.*"

※

Outside the restaurant Will and Gianna leaned against the waterfront railing. The night air was calm but a chill rose from the water and washed over them. She shivered. Finch wondered if he should put an arm around her, but hesitated. When reporters mix professional conduct with romance, disaster is never far behind. Sources always have to be protected — in every conceivable sense. He'd seen more than one story collapse because a key source revealed too much when she (or he) was emotionally vulnerable. It's easy to mistake vulnerability for need, and then misinterpret need for love. Inevitably those missteps lead to denial, and then on-the-record interviews are disputed long after their stories are published. Next, the offended party begins to utter the word "libel." A day or two later the law suits begin to fly.

"You know, something's going on over at the marina," she said. She wrapped her hands over her bare arms and pressed her body against Finch's chest to warm herself.

All right, he thought and inched his chin above her head toward the distant flash of ambulance lights. He inhaled her perfume. Intoxicating. "I think I'm going to drive over to see what's up. You want to come?"

Gianna thought a moment. "No."

"Okay." He looked at her. "You know, I don't think you should drive. Not for another hour or two."

She felt herself sinking into a funk. Was it the Margaritas?

Ray's horrible death? Her family? "I'm going back inside."

"You are?" At first Finch felt an undefined worry, then complete relief. He followed her back to the hostess desk.

Brenda had a puzzled look on her face. "Forget something?"

"No," Finch said. "She needs a pot of strong coffee, a quiet table, and a copy of *People Magazine*."

Gianna forced a laugh. "Right. And more than anything, I need a slice of that dessert you mentioned last week."

"The chocolate bête noir?" Brenda raised her eyebrows.

"Whatever." Gianna leaned over and kissed Finch on the cheek. With her mouth next to his ear, she whispered, "And I'll see you at the Prest later tonight."

He pinched his lips together in a frown. Maybe he couldn't maintain the on-going denial. He wanted her as much as she needed him. But the risk was extreme. If they had a fling she could destroy his career in minutes.

"That's really not a good idea, Gianna," he said. "In fact, it's a very bad idea. Besides, I still have work to do."

CHAPTER NINE

A POLICE BARRICADE blocked the entrance to the wharf and two squad cars were parked bumper-to-bumper to obscure the view looking down into the marina. As Finch pushed forward he could see an ambulance back toward the mouth of the ramp that led onto the pier. The dusk was broken by the pulse of flashing lights. After Gruman's deputy turned Finch away, he waited ten minutes at the sidewalk to assess what was going on.

A fisherman laden with wet netting waddled up from the wharf and through the line of emergency personnel controlling access to the scene below. Finch followed a few steps behind and then overtook him before the old man stepped off the curb.

"Looks like quite a fuss," he said.

"It is." The fisherman studied Finch a moment and nodded. "The *Osprey's Nest* just came in. They pulled a boy up from somewhere past the spit. All tangled up in some line."

"A buoy?" Still puzzled, Finch glanced back at the marina.

"Some kid." He shook his head. "Happens every year. The sheriff says it looks like another accident. Now it's up to them to figure out who he was." He waved a hand at the squad car with a look of relief that this was one job he didn't have to handle.

Finch waited another few minutes then made his way back to the Prest Motel and opened his laptop. Depending on how he wanted to proceed, there might be three stories to write. The first would report the death and necropsy of the black bear. The second would reveal the news of Toeplitz's last meeting with the Whitelaws. The third story he would simply sketch and store on his laptop for now. Ultimately he knew it would be a long feature story describing how Whitelaw's twin boys escorted Toeplitz from their lodge up to Lookout Point on Saddle Mountain where he'd died. With so many unverified elements to the third story, he knew he would have to tread carefully to confirm the damning details. But substantiating testimony would emerge from someone, sometime.

Before he settled down to work he scanned the messages on his phone, cleared the daily text from Bethany ("call me"), checked his laptop for email and searched the online pages of the *eXpress* for any news that Fiona Page might have published. He had a dozen new emails, most of them pro forma notices from the management team: staff scheduling for the pending Memorial Day weekend, a reminder to label your food if storing it in the staff refrigerator. Nothing from Wally and no new message or any news stories from Fiona, except for her on-going coverage of shortages in the Mission district food banks. In other words, all quiet on the home front. He sent Wally and Fiona a joint email: *We have the bear. I sat in on the necropsy. Will file the story within an hour. Also interviewed Gianna Whitelaw today. Toeplitz definitely up here for a meet-*

ing. Toeplitz spent his last day at the family lodge and <u>allegedly</u> was escorted into the hills by the Whitelaw boys. The implications are huge.

He purposely underlined *allegedly,* a word that signified to any journalist that the facts were still disputable. Despite Gianna's recorded testimony, he'd like a second source to verify the twins' culpability before he could claim that they'd escorted Toeplitz to his final destination. Still, Finch believed every word that Gianna had confessed to him and her disclosure pushed the story in a new direction. But even when he added her confession to the other possibilities, the picture of Toeplitz's death seemed unclear.

Furthermore, only a report from the forensics lab could verify that the nine-millimeter slugs and brass were a match — and therefore prove that Toeplitz had been murdered before the bear consumed him. And Jennie Lee wasn't expecting their assessment until tomorrow afternoon. Finch shook his head. That meant delivery sometime late on Sunday, and if the work pace at the forensics lab ran on the typical casual weekend schedule, it could push the report delivery into Monday. For the first time since he'd arrived, he wondered how much longer he could spend in Astoria. He hadn't seen any signs or ads for a local jazz club where he could lose himself for the night. Worrisome.

For the next two hours he set his personal concerns aside and dove into his work. He wrote the report on the bear necropsy from a frontline, I-was-there perspective. Wally used to dismiss this sort of prose as journalistic narcissism, a vestige from the era of Hunter S. Thompson's manic world-view. But

Wally's new mantra — "find the human dimension, not just the facts" — opened the door to first-person feature stories. Finch ripped this story from his memory of the necropsy and put everything onto the page including his collapse on the floor. He considered omitting this bit of personal humiliation, but decided that if readers could feel the visceral heat of the experience, the story would be more powerful. However, he did omit the discovery of the two slugs. That he would save for another day when he could establish a link between the slugs and brass casings.

The second story took considerably longer. Once more he reviewed the sequence of Toeplitz's last days:

• *May 4 at 2 PM in San Francisco the DA announces that he'll depose Toeplitz to support the prosecution in the case of Whitelaw, Whitelaw & Joss*

• *May 5 or 6, Toeplitz departs from SF in his Mercedes GLK*

• *May 7, Toeplitz arrives in Cannon Beach, spends one night at the Whitelaw Lodge*

• *May 8, a Saturday, Toeplitz dies in the switchbacks below Saddle Mountain*

• *May 9, the Argyles come across Toeplitz's corpse*

He then painted a picture of events building the story paragraph by paragraph until he'd written something that seemed both coherent and gripping. He pointed to the many unanswered questions, a vacuum that the reader could only wonder at. Is this really death by misadventure? Or was foul play involved?

When he was done he scanned the notes he'd made about the Whitelaw twins escorting Toeplitz up Saddle Mountain. Finally he sent the first two stories to Jeanine Fix, stood under the shower for ten minutes, and then climbed into bed to read a few pages of a novel he'd picked up in the motel lobby, Dashiell Hammett's *The Thin Man*.

Seconds later his phone rang: Fiona Page.

"Hi. I just got your email about the bear."

"Working Saturday night, are you?"

"Just surfing the net. I got Alexander into bed an hour ago, so...." Her voice hesitated just enough to reveal that she wondered if calling Finch might be a bad idea.

"I'm glad you called," he said. "I just got into bed. What a day."

"Yeah?"

"If things shape up the way I think they will, this story is going to explode."

"What do you mean?"

Finch paused a moment. "Look, you've been terrific digging out the background on this story. But I need to trust you. Completely."

Fiona knew exactly what Finch was driving at. They'd both been burned by fellow colleagues. Finch by a new reporter who claimed not to understand workplace boundaries. Fiona by a gin-soaked veteran who uncovered a memo on her desk and scooped an entire story before she could blink. So much for journalistic ethics. Professional standards were universally proclaimed when it came to maintaining public trust. But protecting your partner? Not so much.

"If you want me to be honest, I can tell you there's *no one* here I can confide in." She offered this in a low voice, as a kind of confession. "If you need someone to trust, and I mean someone to trust *completely*, then yes. But only if it can go both ways."

He shrugged. No surprise. He'd realized years ago that he couldn't fully trust anyone at the old print paper. Except for Wally.

"What about Wally Gimbel?"

"Maybe. If it weren't for his ego. Which is the size of the building."

"True enough. But egos are just like mothers. Everybody has one."

"I guess."

"So do you trust him?"

"… Yes," she hesitated. "He's the managing editor after all. But I don't know that if he'd promised me something and then if the Parson brothers confronted him — I don't know if he'd back me up."

"I've never seen him break his word," Finch assured her. Wally had always helped Finch when he most needed it. But perhaps Fiona was right. If the Parson brothers, joint proprietors of the *Post* and *SF eXpress* applied enough pressure, would Wally crack?

A moment of silence followed and then Fiona continued.

"So, bottom line: you can tell me anything you want and I will treat you as a protected source. I'll never divulge anything for as long as you live."

He laughed. "Impressive, I never thought of myself as a protected source before."

"So tell all," she said.

"All right." Over the next twenty minutes Finch spelled out the details of his visit to the Whitelaw lodge, the bear necropsy, the discovery of the slugs and their possible match with the brass he'd found. He told her about his dinner with Gianna and her revelations about Toeplitz.

"So is she good-looking?"

"Gianna? Not bad." Now he wondered how much to hold back, especially after divulging the most embarrassing details of the necropsy.

"Blonde? Brunette?"

"Brunette." He hesitated. "But she's grieving."

"Therefore in need of a mind-numbing sympathy fuck, I suspect."

Odd. Both woman fixated on sympathy. And sex. "Maybe." Finch laughed and wondered if Gianna would knock on his door anytime soon. He checked the clock. Eleven forty-five. Back at the restaurant he'd said it would be a bad idea. But she seemed to be the determined type. "Look, kiddo, *when you've been in this business as long as I have*" — he laughed again, this time at his preposterous, avuncular tone — "you learn never to mix a story source with a fuck of any kind, least of all out of sympathy."

Fiona chuckled at this and then told him that she had to go. Family commitments: She had to be up by six so she could babysit Alexander's cousin while her sister drove her husband to the airport.

"But call me if you need any help with anything up there, okay?" she said.

"Okay." He sighed, felt another urge to get back to the Bay Area. "I'm glad you called."

"Me too."

He clicked off his phone and thought about the women in his life. Or lack of women. After the smashup with Bethany, he knew that a period of abstinence was in order. But loneliness has a way of clawing at you, of picking at the scab of isolation.

A moment later he heard the light tapping at his door.

❋

"Gianna ... hi." A look of mock surprise fell across Will's face. He'd been expecting her and he knew he'd have to dissuade her from pursuing whatever she had in mind. "Really, this isn't a good idea."

"It's okay, I'm sober now. I promise." Gianna held an arm in the air, fingers crossed as if she were making a false pledge.

"Look, that doesn't change things." He set his hand on the door and leaned against the doorframe to block the entrance to his room. She still wore her black cocktail dress and as she stood beside him, he could see how her body filled the lines of cascading silk, the way her dark hair tumbled in soft curls across her neck. The scoop neckline exposed the taut cleavage of her breasts. Her skin exhaled sweetness and warmth. What a vision.

"This isn't about *that.*" She nodded toward the bed. "It's about our interview."

"What about it?"

"Something's wrong." A narrow pout crossed her lips. "I

just need to talk about it."

He studied her face as he considered his next move. She'd removed her lipstick and the rims of her eyes appeared puffy and sore. Obviously she'd been crying.

"Can I come in? Please." She raised her open hands, a plea for sympathy. "Just for ten minutes."

"All right. But just ten." Finch shook his head in a gesture of concession and dropped his arm from the door. Part of him felt exasperated. Another part, desire.

"Thanks." She brushed against his chest as she passed into the room. She glanced at the bed and the two chairs. "They haven't redecorated these little bed-stalls since my grad night."

"Which would be when? Two, maybe three years ago?" He threw off this compliment with a smile but a dim anxiety gnawed at his stomach.

"Yeah. Sure." She laughed. "Closer to twelve or thirteen. But I like to pretend. One of my personal flaws, apparently."

"Have a seat, Gianna." His hand swept toward the plastic chair beside the bedside table.

She squeezed past him and sat down, then tucked the edges of her dress under her thighs and brushed her hair over a shoulder. He sat opposite her in the tiny space next to the bed and leaned forward and set his hands on his knees. "So, you're worried about the interview." He laid this out as a matter of fact. "It's not uncommon. Happens a lot, actually."

"That's just it." Her voice came as whisper. "You can't print it. You can't print anything I said tonight."

Finch leaned forward and tried to catch her eyes. "So what's changed, Gianna? A few hours ago, you said I could ask you anything and that you wouldn't respond to something if you didn't want to. So who's changed your mind?"

"No one's changed my mind." Her voice raised a notch. "It's just … I can't.…"

He let her words drift a moment, then pressed forward. "Can't what, Gianna?"

She stood up as if she wanted to leave, then seemed to decide that she had nowhere to go. She turned and settled on the edge of the bed facing him. "No one should know all that. About Raymond. About my brothers. *About what happened.*"

When he saw tears brimming in her eyes, he realized her story was only half completed. She had more to reveal, but couldn't bring herself to tell all. Maybe he could prompt her with a little coaxing. "So what *did* happen, Gianna?"

"Nothing." She held a finger to her lips as if she were holding back an enormous secret — one she desperately wanted to reveal. But at the moment when she was about to unlock the mystery, two tears rolled down her cheeks, one from each eye.

"Gianna." A wave of compassion swept through him. He felt responsible, protective, needed. "Come on. No need for that." He sat beside her and slipped an arm behind her waist.

"I'm sorry," she muttered and brushed away her tears. "I promised myself I wouldn't do this. I'm such a fucking mess right now."

"It's okay. Everyone understands what you've been through." His hand slid up to her bare shoulder. Her skin was silk.

"Oh please," she moaned and turned and rolled against his

chest as her arms wrapped around his back. She looked up at him and kissed his mouth. "I need this so much," she said and kissed him again.

※

They dozed, but after an hour Gianna shifted her head from Finch's shoulder. She propped her chin into the palm of her hand. She gazed at Finch's unblemished face. "You *are* handsome, you know."

"What's that?" He tried to blink away the sleep enveloping him.

"For a journalist, I mean." She kissed his forehead and ran her hand over his chest. "And ballsy. The way you walked into the kitchen, sat at Daddy's table like you belonged there." She pressed her lips to his shoulder. "For a moment you made me forget about Raymond. I wanted to ride you right there." She kissed him again and climbed out of the bed.

"Are you leaving?"

"I have to get back to San Fran."

"What?"

"I'll text you when I get there." She waved a business card in the air. "I've got the cell number on your card."

"Are you serious?" He pushed away from the pillows. "You're leaving now?"

"Yes, now. I told my father I was getting out. Today. *Yesterday,*" she corrected herself as she slipped into her dress. "I realize it's the only thing I can do to get my life back. A final break from my family. All of them, except my mother. You helped me figure it out, Will. Tonight — right now!" Her shoes slid onto her feet. "And *you* definitely have to see me again.

138

Okay?"

He stared at her in disbelief. What had come so unexpectedly, now departed too soon.

"Okay?" Her voice held an edge of desperation.

"Yeah. The day I get back," he murmured. He tried to muster up a mental image of his daily calendar, his place in time. "Sometime next week."

She paused at the door, a moment of deliberation. She took a step back toward him and said, "By the way, you can do it if you want."

"Do what?"

"Publish the story. Everything I said tonight. Everything we talked about. It's the only way the truth will get out."

He nodded. Did she know that he'd publish it no matter what she'd said? No matter how much she might plead.

"All right. I will."

"Good." She blew him a kiss and was gone.

CHAPTER TEN

JENNIE LEE HUNCHED at her desk and stared at the computer. The digital clock at the top of the screen read 1:34 AM. She wondered if she snatched two or three hours of sleep now, would she have enough time to finish the autopsy report and slap it onto Gruman's desk by ten in the morning. She'd never seen him so agitated as he marched back and forth across the parking lot in front of the marina earlier that evening. He'd turned the case into a personal crusade to get to the bottom of the incident that had claimed the boy's life. "*Miss* Jennie Lee," he'd barked once the corpse was on the trolley and headed toward the ambulance, "I want your report on my desk by noon tomorrow. No, damn it — I want it by ten A.M."

Damn, what a hardass.

She decided to break her resolution against ordering pizza from Sahara Pizza on weekends. On weekdays, when she might work all hours, a slice of pizza was permissible, but weekends when she could prepare a sensible salad? Forbidden.

"Make it a vegetarian, double-cheese, no mushrooms," she sighed through the phone.

"Be there in twenty minutes," the pizza boy claimed, but

from past experience she knew not to set her watch by it. Among so many other annoyances, the pace of pizza delivery in Astoria made her homesick for Portland. Back home, if pizza was delivered even a minute late it was free.

But twenty minutes would give her time to digest what she'd discovered about her latest John Doe, aged fifteen to seventeen. She knew she needed to clear her mind and focus. Apart from the ligature marks around his wrist where he'd grasped the cord attached to the prawn trap, the body was free of any marks, abrasions or wounds. In addition, the autopsy revealed the classic symptoms of death by drowning. In fact, this was a textbook case: sufficient water in the lungs to block the flow of oxygen to the brain leading to brain death, probably within about six minutes of immersion. Cardiac arrest likely followed within another few minutes. Because water was found in the stomach *and* in the lungs, the victim was probably alive when he fell into the sea. Following his immersion into the ocean a predictable sequence of responses followed: water splashed into the mouth, the gag reflex led to gasping for air, and water ran down the boy's gullet into his stomach. Since rigor mortis had already subsided, she'd have to make a guess about the date of death. The corpse was only moderately decomposed and relatively free of scavenger bites, except those to his face which rendered him unrecognizable. Therefore, she assumed he'd died less than two days ago. She could only conclude that the boy had drowned as the result of an accident in which he'd become entangled in a prawn trap as it was being hauled onto, or cast off, from a boat. Once the forensics staff and the sheriff confirmed his identity, the sheriff's team would perform a routine canvass of the victim's friends and associates to determine who'd seen him last and "the circumstances of the accident." Once again, Gruman's words. Words that haunted her.

And therein lay the heart of Jennie Lee's moody funk. Once her report was submitted, the forensic results of the case would determine the course of action. And this particular John Doe provided a maze of forensic puzzle pieces. Item one: a relatively new Glock 19 G4 9mm with a partially loaded magazine cinched under the belt of the victim. Item two: the empty prawn trap attached to a quarter-inch-thick nylon line. The cable, still firmly in the grip of John Doe's left hand as he was hauled onto the deck of the *Osprey Nest*, was entangled in the ship's nets as it passed through Clatsop Spit. The ship's captain, Wesley Mann, had the good sense not to unravel anything attached to the corpse, the cord, or the prawn trap.

When Jennie and Gruman had arrived on the deck of the *Osprey Nest*, the forensics team had already photographed and documented the tangled mess that Wesley Mann had hauled aboard his boat. After inspecting the situation and following all necessary protocols, Gruman gave the all-clear and assigned the grim tasks ahead to each party. The body was loaded into the ambulance and driven to the pit where Jennie completed the autopsy. The Glock and the prawn trap were allotted to the deputy sheriff, Biff Winslow. He was Gruman's old school friend and the sheriff trusted Winslow to handle the grizzly details of all the county's dead and dismembered tragedies.

"Give priority to the Glock," Gruman had said to Winslow, his face in a scowl. "I want to know the history of that gun right down to the name of the Nazi-Austrian son-of-a-bitch who designed the trigger on the damn thing."

Winslow had smiled, unsure if Gruman was joking. He'd seen the sheriff's temper blow hot and cold many times, often as the lead-up to a joke.

"I'm not fucking kidding." Gruman had narrowed his eyes when he saw the disbelief in Winslow's face.

"All right." Winslow shrugged, secured the pistol and carefully set it in his kit bag. "Then I'll see about this prawn trap and the line."

"Whatever," Gruman had said and turned his attention to the men climbing off the *Osprey Nest*.

Jennie then watched Deputy Winslow coil the line that led to the trap and noticed a look of surprise cross his face as he peered at the brass plate fixed to the empty trap.

"Jesus. Mark, get over here and take a look at this."

Gruman turned back to his friend and gazed at the name plate on the trap. Jennie had seen his face blanch as the blood drained from his cheeks.

Biff Winslow then uttered something in a whisper that Jennie could not decipher.

Both of them had glanced at Jennie.

"All right. Back to work, everyone." Gruman barked.

When Jennie hesitated, he took a step toward her. It marked a turning point, she now realized. That's when he'd said, his voice coiled and rattling, "*Miss* Jennie Lee, I want your report on my desk by noon tomorrow. No, damn it — I want it by ten AM."

What a hardass.

143

※

"No, there's no word about the nine millimeter slugs and the brass. I told you we wouldn't get that until this afternoon. At the earliest. And with the drowning last night, we'll probably have to wait until next week for any more news."

Jennie rubbed her eyes and sipped her coffee. She hadn't felt this tired since she'd been in med school back in Portland. She'd agreed to meet Finch for breakfast only if she could choose the restaurant. The Astoria Coffee House and Bistro was usually quiet in the morning and she knew they could speak in confidence.

"Besides, Biff Winslow was side-tracked by the sheriff," she continued in order to explain the potential delays ahead. "Gruman told him to put all other investigations aside until he ID'ed the owner of the Glock."

"Biff Winslow? Who is Biff Winslow?" Finch swallowed the last bit of his breakfast and pushed his plate aside. "And, more important, why do half the people up here sound as if they were named after an uncle in the Ozarks?"

Jennie laughed, felt the first glimmer of levity since Thursday when Finch crash-landed next to the examining table in the pit.

"The deputy sheriff," she said and wondered if she should reveal his decades-old friendship with Gruman. "Besides Gruman, he's one of the few paid cops in the county. Everyone else is deputized whenever they're needed. Which is at least once a month, from what I can tell."

"Okay, I get it. The drowning of a local kid takes priority over a week-old bear attack on some blue-suit, out-of-towner like Toeplitz. And I know this sounds heartless of me, but *sorry*, it's getting in the way of the story I'm working on."

Finch set his jaw and frowned at Jennie. For the past ten minutes he'd listened to her monologue about the boy, just identified as Donnel Smeardon, who'd been fished out of the ocean by the crew on the *Osprey Nest*. Not only had the drowning troubled her — she felt it whenever a young life was cut short — but the sheriff had responded with such an iron-fisted pique that she couldn't sleep even after she'd finished her report. But to Finch, the only interesting element to her story was news of the Glock.

"By the way, that's two of us," he said, "who didn't get much sleep. I spent half the night piecing together Toeplitz's murder." His mind turned to Gianna. Best not to mention her to Jennie.

Jennie's face clouded over. She seemed distracted by the puzzles presented by Donnel Smeardon's drowning.

"With what we now know about the nine-mille slugs," he said as he leaned forward to ensure he had her attention, "it's all completely obvious."

He let this hang. When Jennie didn't offer a response, he continued.

"Toeplitz is driving up Saddle Mountain. Someone, and I'll get to *who* in a minute, pulls him to a stop at the side of the road. He opens the car window. That someone approaches and without warning fires two slugs point blank into his chest or head. We'll never know exactly where he was struck according to your autopsy, but the important point is that Toeplitz is left to bleed-out in his Mercedes. That accounts for your concern about the volume of blood found in the car and it proves that the bear didn't attack him and immediately drag him through the window. Next, the killer flees the scene. And as dumb luck would have it, twenty or thirty minutes later the bear ambles down the road. He stands, sniffs the air and discovers Toeplitz's corpse. After a brief struggle, the bear claws at the door and finally manages to wrench Toeplitz out of the open window. The bear drags him up the road to a place where he feels secure, where he can watch for other predators. Then … the rest happens." Will waved a hand and glanced away.

Jennie nodded. "All right."

"Now the next act in the tragedy unfolds. Ethan and Ben Argyle happen to walk down to the road hunting for deer. They see the abandoned Mercedes and fifty yards along, our bear. The rest, once again, we know."

"Okay. Now who's the *someone*?"

Finch propped his elbows on the table and leaned even closer. "The some *one*, is in fact *two* people."

"Two?" She shook her head.

"Justin and Evan Whitelaw, age twenty-seven. Positioned to move up the ranks at the Senator's firm," he added. "It turns out that on the morning of Toeplitz's death, they drove him out to Saddle Mountain. They went in two cars. One of the boys accompanied Toeplitz, the other led the way in his own car."

"Are you sure about this?"

"It's all on here." Finch held his phone aloft as if it were a legal exhibit. "From an interview I took last night."

A puzzled look crossed her face. "With who?"

Finch considered this. If Gianna hadn't come to his room

146

last night, he'd have no reason to withhold this information. "Protection of sources. I simply can't disclose that. Not yet, anyway. Now," he paused, scanned the room, and continued, "here's my theory of how it went down. The two cars are traveling up the switchbacks on the mountainside, Justin leading the way, Toeplitz and Evan following. It's all a set-up because Toeplitz had wanted to see the area for years but never took the time before. The idea is that they'll drive up to the summit, take in the view, and when it's time for Toeplitz to head back to San Francisco, he'll drive east on route 26 and the twins will return to the lodge in Cannon Beach."

"It sounds like an obvious setup. I mean, wouldn't Toeplitz suspect something? Given all the tension between them, why would he get in a car with them?"

"Not with his condition."

"Which is what?"

"Asperger's Syndrome. Apparently he hid it well, but he couldn't decode any complicated social situations." Finch leaned back in the chair now and took a last sip of his Americano. "I have a friend with the same affliction. It's a remarkable combination of intelligence and social dysfunction." He looked at her and felt a tinge of embarrassment. "Of course you know all that."

Jennie let this pass. A worried look crossed her face. Finch's theory explained a lot of her own concerns, but she wanted to find the holes in it. She'd need to have answers to any questions that Gruman would put to her about launching a formal inquest.

"If he hid his Asperger's so well, how did your source

know about it?"

Finch smiled and held up his phone again. He remembered the words the senator had used to scold his daughter: that she and Toeplitz were *joined at the hip.* "That's protected, too."

She looked across the restaurant to the cashier. The breakfast crowd was moving on and the room was now almost empty.

"So what do you need to launch an inquest, Jennie? We've established the criminal means and opportunity, and I have on record a witness who saw Justin and Evan Whitelaw leave with Toeplitz in two separate cars. Then that evening the boys returned together in one vehicle."

She narrowed her eyes. She had one more question, one to which she already knew the answer. "And their motive?"

Finch frowned. How could she bother to ask? "To eliminate the one person who could send the partners in Whitelaw, Whitelaw & Joss to jail for twenty years."

She nodded. *"If* the forensic report shows that the slugs we found in the bear match the brass you found on the road, then I'll go to Gruman and demand an investigation. *If,"* she repeated.

"And if he blocks you?"

She thought a moment. "Then I'll go above him. To the Oregon State Police."

CHAPTER ELEVEN

MARK GRUMAN PARKED the police cruiser in front of the Argyle house and cut the ignition. There were a lot of approaches he could take to this visit and on the drive over from the county sheriff's office he'd decided to play the gentleman's game.

There'd been a lot of uneasy tension between him and Ethan Argyle over the decades, nothing ever overt, nothing that ever caused Gruman to employ any of the legal authority empowered by his position. The tension, whatever remained of it, came from their teenage years at Astoria High School. Millie Pitt, once Gruman's girlfriend, had gone off to Portland for the summer following their tenth grade. When she came back, she'd told him that she didn't want to see him in September. Gruman assumed she'd met someone and that she'd made a long-distant commitment to this dude, whoever he was. Her estrangement lasted until the Christmas holidays. Then it dawned on Gruman that Millie Pitt had given her affection to Ethan Argyle, a local boy two years older than Millie, who'd returned from his first term at Oregon State University.

Gruman knew that the gentleman's game also dictated the charade he now had to play. The Glock found on Donnel

Smeardon's corpse was the same pistol he'd confiscated from the boy the night he apprehended him during the drug bust at Jackie Spitzer's. The same pistol he'd returned to Smeardon during the run out to Clatsop Spit on the *Gold Coaster.* The same pistol owned by Ethan Argyle — and jacked by his own son, Ben — to satisfy some unknown obligation Ben owed Donnel Smeardon. Could Ben also be ensnared in Smeardon's pot smuggling schemes?

No, not likely. Gruman exhaled two long plumes of smoke from his nostrils and crushed the butt of his Lucky Strike in the cruiser's ashtray. Still, it would be worth seeing the look of doubt on the faces of Ethan and Millie Argyle when he presented them with the fact that their love child stood at the center of some serious misdemeanor. Or even — he let this thought hang in his mind as he walked toward their doorstep — a possible felony.

"I hope I'm not disturbing your lunch hour," he said to Ethan and Millie after she'd served them coffee and a plate of freshly baked banana bread. He stretched out his legs under the coffee table and examined the living room fireplace. The high-efficiency insert glowed with a dry warmth that insulated the house from the damp air flowing in from the Pacific. A load of quartered fir logs lay stacked against the brick wall next to the fireplace. Enough fuel to last a week. Gruman assumed another two or three cords of wood were stored under the eavestrough outside the house.

"No. At least not today." Millie frowned, a look that suggested she still bore some disdain for him. And her memory of him.

"Tell me, is Ben at home?"

"He's at the school gym." A note of tension lifted Ethan's voice. Until now, there'd been an outside possibility that Gruman could be making a purely social call.

"Mmm." He nodded. "Perhaps that's just as well." He let this idea settle as he smiled at Millie.

She couldn't return his simpering look. "Mark, has something happened to Ben?"

"No." He waved a hand to suggest he didn't mean to alarm them. "Hell, *no*. Nothing too serious." He smiled. "Well, I hope not, anyway."

"Mark," Ethan said and leaned forward, "what are you saying?"

"Ah, damn it." He shook his head and slapped both hands onto his thighs. "Let me get right to the point. Ethan, as I remember, you own a Glock nine-millimeter pistol, right?"

A look of surprise crossed Ethan's face. "Yes. I've got it locked up in the gun room."

"Do you?"

"Yes."

He studied Ethan's face. "A half an hour ago Biff Winslow identified a Glock 9 that was found on the corpse of Donnel Smeardon."

"Donnel Smeardon?" Millie gasped and glanced across the room. "Is that who was found out in the spit last night?"

Gruman turned his attention to her and nodded. He tried to sense what she might be feeling but he couldn't decipher the grimace of shock on her face. A look of emptiness. Of bleakness. What could Donnel Smeardon mean to her?

"Did you know him?"

"I met him just the once." Her voice drained into a vacant whisper. "Ben had him over one afternoon."

"A few weeks ago," Ethan added.

"You knew him too?"

"Knew him? No. He's a student at the school, but not in any of my classes." Ethan shook his head. "What does this have to do with my Glock?"

"I'm not sure. Not yet, anyway." He pulled two photographs from his pocket and laid them on the coffee table. One was of a Glock 9, the other a close-up showing the pistol's serial number. "Are these familiar?"

Ethan lifted the image of the serial number in his right hand and frowned. He couldn't remember the exact numerical sequence, but this was damn close. "It might be," he allowed.

Gruman tipped his head to one side. "If it is, then your gun was found on Smeardon's body when he was hauled onto the *Osprey Nest*."

"I can't see how that's possible." Ethan shook his head. "Let me get it. I'll show you." He stood and looked around the room, stumbled a moment as if he weren't sure where the gun room might be.

"Do you mind if I come with you?" Gruman stood and took a step forward.

Ethan waved a hand in the air. "Sure. Of course." A feeling of indecision ebbed through him. As he walked down the hallway past the kitchen his mind flooded with doubts. Where was the key? Where was the gun? *Where was Ben?*

When a sense of purpose returned, he drew the gun room

key from his desk drawer and led Gruman to the locked closet near the garage. The door opened and he clicked on the light. The room was little more than a sealed cubical. On the wall facing them stood a rack housing six guns of various types and vintage. The two Winchester rifles that he and Ben had used on Saddle Mountain, two matching Benelli shot guns and two AR-15s. Ethan tested the cage with his hand to ensure it was secure.

"You ever fire those 15s?" Gruman rolled his tongue over his teeth.

"Once or twice a month." He was surprised by the question. Gruman and Ethan belonged to the same gun club; the members shared the same views of gun ownership and maintenance.

"What about the pistols?"

Ethan pointed at the locked drawer beneath the gun rack. He hesitated, turned the key and then opened it a few inches. When he saw that the Glock was missing he drew an audible breath. "Shit."

"Ethan, I've got to ask you this. It's just procedure. Did you give your Glock 9 to Donnel Smeardon?"

"Of course not."

"All right. What about the ammo?" Gruman's voice was flat, steady. The same tone he'd use if he was setting the hook on a big fish he'd been waiting for years to reel in. No need to dramatize. He'd already shredded Argyle's story and with his denial, Gruman could now build the link to the gun found on Smeardon through his son. He'd snagged Argyle and he could play him any way he wanted.

"In the bedroom." Ethan closed the door to the gun room,

locked it and led Gruman to his bedroom, then to the walk-in closet and a safe which was bolted to the floor and wall. He spun the cylinder, swung open the steel case door and examined the inventory. "Looks like everything's here."

"Good." Gruman studied the safe with disinterest. He had no legal need to verify that the ammunition was secured. Instead he studied the shirts, pants, dresses, sweaters, all hung in neat rows around them. He stepped back into the bedroom and examined the furniture. A queen bed with maple head- and footboards, a matching dresser and highboy, matching night tables — everything of a piece. And all in good order. No likelihood of kinky sex here. He tried to imagine living the lives that ghosted through this house. He frowned, content with the vacant mood of the room.

"You've got my pistol, then?"

"We have to keep it for a while." Gruman shrugged to suggest that the disposition of the gun extended beyond his power.

Sensing that Gruman might stand in his bedroom for a long while, Ethan led the way back to the living room. Millie still sat in her chair, her eyes glazed with a look of disbelief.

"It's gone," he whispered to her and glanced away, unable to explain how the pistol had come into the possession of the odd boy who Ben had brought to their house one rainy afternoon.

"What happens now?" He didn't want to sit again. Better that Gruman move on and let them sort out the situation on their own when Ben returned.

"We'll track down Donnel Smeardon's activities over the

past week." He pressed his lips together. "See what it was that led to his drowning. Though that's not always easy," he added.

"Seems every year we lose someone out there." Millie nodded in the direction of the ocean.

"Drowning's the most common cause of death for adolescents," Gruman said. "In any case, we have no evidence that your pistol was used in any way out of the ordinary. Not yet, anyway."

Ethan walked towards the front door.

Gruman paused and looked down at Millie. He wondered about their high school years, wondered if he ever truly felt anything for her. Most likely not.

"Let me know if we can do anything to help you out with this." Ethan swung the front door open. The moist breeze filled the hallway.

"I will." Gruman walked away without smiling. "And tell Ben to call me as soon as he gets home. I need to talk to him so we can put this thing to rest."

※

Ethan closed the door, and from the window he watched Gruman climb into his squad car, drive along the road and out of sight. His stomach felt empty and the emptiness knotted his belly. When he turned back to where Millie sat on the love seat, he saw her eyes welling with tears.

"Millie?" He took two steps toward her and stopped when she averted her face from him.

"It's nothing," she said and waved him away with a hand.

"It's not nothing. I can hear it in your voice. And it's more than the news about Donnel Smeardon," he added, and walked to the loveseat and placed a hand on her shoulder.

She brushed the tears from her face and looked at her husband. She forced a smile to her lips. "I guess I'm worried about Ben. He's done so well. The scholarship to Stanford — but now this. It could wreck everything."

"Not if he's *not* involved." He shook his head with certainty. "I mean how could he be involved with this?"

Millie studied the fire through the glass door on the wood stove, tried to absorb the warmth radiating through the room. "Ben doesn't need to be involved. Unless Mark Gruman decides to *make* him involved."

Ethan walked past his wife and sat on the sofa facing her. "What are you saying?" He shook his head. "I don't quite get it."

Millie drew a long breath and tried to explain. But before she could utter a word, she broke into tears and began sobbing.

"Millie." Ethan moved back to the love seat and sat beside his wife. His arm slipped over her shoulders and he pulled her against his chest. "What is it, darling? What's all this?"

She took a moment to find her breath, surprised that she was so overwhelmed. How could this have festered so long without her acknowledging it? How could the old pain, buried so deep, pierce her now and with such force?

"Look, Ben's going to be okay. I'm sure of it." Ethan pressed his forehead against her hair, inhaled her scent.

"I know," she said with a light gasp. "It's not about Ben."

"Well, whatever this is, you have to tell me," he whispered. "I've never seen you like this."

She waited another moment and swallowed what she could

of the pain. "It's Mark Gruman."

Ethan pulled his head away from her, a slight movement, an adjustment so that he could hear what was coming.

"You remember. Before we first met."

He nodded. "It was a high school thing. You'd just broken up with him."

"And he promised me something." But that was after what happened, she told herself. The promise came after what really happened.

"He promised you something?"

She had to pause again. Had to wait for the sequence of events to line up properly, the order of humiliations that destroyed the delicate part of her that night. "The day we broke up, the night I told him I couldn't go on with him any more, he made me a promise. 'One day Millie, I will hurt you the way you tried to hurt me. I promise you that. I will *hurt* you.' He said all that. Word for word."

Ethan took her face in his hand and looked at her eyes. He could see it there, a suffering so deep that she couldn't describe it to him. "He hurt you then, didn't he?"

She nodded and looked away. Then she felt the release of the torment she'd buried so deep for so long. She turned her eyes to his and felt the tears course down her cheeks. "Yes. He did," she said. "He hurt me so badly, I could never tell you before."

They sat together in silence, listening to the sounds of hot coals popping in the fireplace, quietly settling their bodies into one another — an old habit now renewed.

"He raped you, didn't he."

157

She nodded against his shoulder. "Yes." A whisper.

He pressed her head to his cheek, felt her tears on his face. "I'm glad you told me, Mill. I can't believe you kept it to yourself so long."

As he held her, he stared at the fire pawing at the glass of the wood stove door and wondered how things would turn out now. How he could drive this misery out of their home. And when.

CHAPTER TWELVE

AFTER HIS BREAKFAST meeting with Jennie, Will returned to his motel room and began to compile background notes on Franklin Whitelaw's twin sons, Justin and Evan. The internet, awash with thousands of entries on the boys, provided a gallery view of California's elite. Following their birth to Whitelaw's second wife (a former starlet who'd spoken no more than three lines in a dozen forgettable B-movies), the twins emerged as a symbol of the family's unique brand of celebrity, wealth, power, good looks, and unrelenting self-esteem. Over twenty years a photograph of the boys appeared in the press once or twice a month. As the internet evolved, they became more prominent. Facebook provided a continuous flow of their personal escapades. Several of the boys' friends and girlfriends published completely accessible gossip, rumors, photos and videos of the twins' antics through their high school and college years. They thrived on the edge of scandal and excess.

But neither of them crashed through the thin restraints of what Finch called YMS: Young Male Syndrome. If they'd committed crimes and misdemeanors, these had been covered up — by a pro. Dozens of entries about the other Whitelaw children appeared alongside many of these postings, including glimpses of Gianna and her mother, Sophia, Whitelaw's first wife. Gianna had enjoyed her parties, too, and the most recent Facebook tags included images of Gianna draped around the unsmiling Raymond Toeplitz.

The latest gossip about Whitelaw's teenage daughters, Terri and Melody, from his third and current wife, focused on their shopping sprees on Rodeo Drive. Twenty-thousand dollars in clothes. Their mother, Sassy, grinned in the background next to a cash register. Must be fun to clutch the senator's Amex card in one hand and the keys to his Mercedes in the other. After a few hours, Finch leaned back in his chair and pitched a few headlines that would introduce his feature article. *The Kennedys of California.* Better still, *The Bushes of Berkeley Hills.*

A little after noon Finch decided to send Fiona an email. He wanted to attach the backgrounder he'd prepared and ask her to follow up with anything she could uncover that would broaden the picture of the twins. But what he'd written seemed too clean. Not that he needed more dirt to pile on the legal case the prosecutor had built against the family firm. No, Finch had a deeper concern. All the frat house pranks, the rumors of orgies, drugs and booze were ultimately benign. Nothing in their very public history suggested the boys were capable of planning and executing a cold-blooded killing. They were party boys, not hit men. He needed at least a hint that they traveled somewhere on the dark side. Maybe Fiona could dig deeper into their private world and unearth their secret story.

Before he could send the message, his phone rang: Jennie

Lee.

"Hi Jennie, what's up?" He pushed his laptop aside and pressed his back against the bed pillows.

"It's a match. The slugs from the bear and the brass you found on the road. Winslow just told me." Her voice came in light, uneven panting. "He said the ballistics expert figures the probability is above ninety percent."

Finch's shoulders relaxed. His belly softened. "Biff Winslow, the deputy sheriff?"

"Yes."

"All right. But look, neither of us should be surprised. Ninety percent isn't a lock-down, but it's close enough for you to request a formal inquest, isn't it?"

"It should be."

"Jennie, where are you?"

"On the ridge trail. Same place we were walking on Wednesday. I had to get out for a run to clear my head."

Finch glanced through the window. A steady drizzle tapped against the glass. "In this weather?"

"Look, there's more to this than either of us thought."

Finch waited for her to continue. He knew the pattern: whenever she had new information, she needed to assess what part she could reveal to him. He realized she needed another prod.

"Jennie, I didn't have to tell you about the Whitelaw's sons escorting Toeplitz up to Saddle Mountain. Or about the bullet casings I found. I could simply have published—"

"Have you?"

"Have I what?"

"Published that story. Because if you did, you're wrong. At least about the Whitelaws."

Finch paused. "All right. So tell me what you know."

"This is from Biff Winslow but he won't put any of it in writing. Not yet, any way. So this is off the record, okay?"

Finch took a moment to consider this. She knew all the rules and knew that he would play by them. "Okay."

"This morning I told you about a boy found drowned off the mouth of the river. That the sheriff found a gun on his body."

Finch nodded. "A Glock."

"*Look, this is so far off the record....* Jesus, I shouldn't be telling you any of this."

"Listen, Jennie," Finch stared at the motel wall. "Here's what I think. One of the reasons you're telling me what you have is because you're frightened. And you're frightened because this case is unlike anything you've seen before. Believe me, I know what that's like." He turned his chin to one side as he recalled the first story that had eaten into his soul. "I promise you this. I will never reveal that you are the source of whatever you tell me for as long as I live."

A moment of silence filled the air.

"All right." She lowered her voice to a barely audible whisper. "The bullets that killed Raymond Toeplitz were fired from from the Glock found on Donnel Smeardon. But here's the kicker. Winslow and Gruman know everyone in the county. Unlikely as it sounds, Winslow told me the only person he knows who owns a nine-mille Glock is Ethan Argyle."

Finch tapped a finger on his lips. "Ben Argyle's father?"

"One and the same."

Finch scanned the ceiling as he tried to align the puzzle pieces. "So … where does that leave us?" He was thinking out loud now. He knew it was a sign that his story might be falling to pieces.

"I don't know."

Finch's mind began to race through the possibilities. "Well, it leaves us with the Whitelaw twins one step removed from actually pulling the trigger. But, they could still have been there. Just like the bear."

"I don't know." Jennie sounded doubtful. "What about motive? Why would a kid, either Smeardon or Ben Argyle shoot Toeplitz? It's unlikely they ever met him."

Finch held a hand in the air. "Hold on, you mean no motive that we can see. Not yet, anyway."

"What about Ethan Argyle?" Jennie asked. "If he actually owns the gun, we can't dismiss him, either."

Finch shook his head. The father seemed even more unlikely. He had a family, a good job. "Does he have any criminal history?"

"I doubt it. Gruman will be checking that, but they're both from Astoria. They're all second cousins out here."

Finch laughed. True enough. This end of the gene pool seemed pretty damn shallow.

"Look I've got to go." Her heavy breathing had subsided. Finch imagined that she was now preparing to jog across the top of Saddle Mountain.

"Okay."

"So we're back to square one."

"Not really." Finch pouted and rubbed a finger over his lip. "When this kind of thing happens, you just have to reframe the facts. Once you get that right, the picture clarifies."

"Well let me know when your vision's back to twenty-twenty." Jennie's voice carried a note of sarcasm. "I've got a lot to do."

"Okay. And tell me when you start the inquest."

She hung up without a response and Finch tossed his phone to the far end of the bed. What a bloody mess.

CHAPTER THIRTEEN

"I'M GOING TO face this on my own!" Ben shouted and then dropped his head into his hands.

"I don't know that you *can*." Ethan narrowed his eyes and considered the tears and remorse flooding through his son. Millie had already fled to the sanctuary of the bedroom when she saw her husband clenching his fists. And when Ben began to choke on his own sobbing, Ethan knew it was time to lower the heat. The two of them had gone at it for ten minutes as soon as the boy returned from basketball practice after school. Not a dog fight, but still, probably the worst argument they'd had.

"Yes, I can," Ben insisted when he recovered. He sat in a chair at the kitchen table, and lifted his head to look at his father. "With Donnel dead, it's one thing I *have* to do. Go in there and talk to Sheriff Gruman on my own."

What could that possibly mean? Ethan paced in front of the table. He realized there had to be more to the missing pistol than mere theft. "All right, but I want to know how Donnel Smeardon died with my pistol in his possession."

"I don't know the answer to that. Three days ago he didn't even have the gun."

"What?" Ethan shook his head in disbelief. "And how do you know *that?*"

Ben hated the look on his father's face. "Okay. Before that … I gave the pistol to Donnel."

"*You* did."

"That's all I can tell you right now." He stood up and walked to the far end of the kitchen. He couldn't explain why he gave the Glock to Donnel Smeardon. There was something crazy to it all that he didn't understand. An impulse. A desire to have Donnel boast what a stand-up dude Ben Argyle was. None of it made sense.

When Ben realized that his father had accepted this last statement, he cut through the back door, jumped on his mountain bike and pedaled toward the Sheriff's office on Seventh. Ten minutes later he leaned the bike against the building wall, locked it and pressed his teeth together until they hurt. As he walked into the building he realized it was better he'd already had it out with his mother and father. That way Sheriff Gruman couldn't hold the threat of parental disgrace against him, too. Despite the relief, he could still feel the adrenaline coursing through his body and he felt the sinews cramping in his arms and legs. *Do not fuck with me,* he whispered to himself.

The interior of the station appeared to be half-empty, almost abandoned. He stood next to an area marked RECEPTION where Mary-Beth Wheeler talked on a phone at her desk. In front of her a long wood counter blocked off access to the center of the office and two rows of six workstations. One desk was occupied by an officer Ben did not recognize, the others were vacant and coated with a layer of dust. Before Mary-Beth could acknowledge him, Gruman appeared from an office door at the far end of the room and pointed a finger at him and clicked his thumb. Pistol-shot.

"Over here, Ben." His voice was flat, but loud enough to carry the length of the building. He disappeared back into the office.

"Yessir," Ben said and cursed himself. Mary-Beth pressed a concealed button and a gate in the middle of the counter popped open an inch. He pushed through it, swung it back in place and made his way to the sheriff's office.

"Close the door," Gruman said without looking up from his chair.

Ben shut the door and glanced around the workplace. The building, a designated heritage site, had always seemed pleasant enough to Ben from the outside, but the interior reeked of age and slow-motion collapse. He sat in a metal chair opposite Gruman's massive desk which was littered with stacks of files, books, photographs, newspapers — a jumble of chaos that caught Ben by surprise. This mess belongs to the county sheriff?

"Try to ignore this." Gruman waved a hand at the clutter. "This is what happens when the economy goes south. We've been cut back and understaffed here for three years. Everybody left has taken salary cuts, including me."

Ben shrugged.

"I guess that wouldn't matter to someone your age." He applied a smile to his lips and decided to change gears. "I appreciate you coming in, Ben. I'm sure it wasn't pleasant getting the news from your father and Millie."

Ben turned his head aside. Another surprise: he knew his mother as Millie?

"I know them both pretty well. We all went though AHS together." He narrowed his eyes to take in the boy. Once again, there were so many ways to play this. "You kids still pronounce it *awes?*"

"Some do." He drew a long breath.

Gruman nodded. Now that Ben had spoken, the weight of silence would fall on him. The sheriff stood up, took a key from his pocket and opened a locked vault behind his desk. From there he extracted an evidence bag and set it in front of the boy. He pushed some papers from the side of the desk, plumped his left thigh onto the wood surface, stared down at him and waited.

"So that's it."

"Look familiar?"

Ben hesitated.

"Go ahead. It's not loaded. Not any more."

He lifted the opaque bag in his hand, pulled the plastic tight against the pistol grip. "I guess so."

"No, Ben." Gruman adjusted his weight on the desk. "There's no guessing involved. That's your father's pistol. Now what we all need to know — and by *we*, I mean me, your father and the prosecutor — what *we* need to know is how this gun came to sit here in front of you at this very moment in time."

Ben tried to swallow. He could barely open his mouth. "May I have some water?"

May I? Gruman shook his head and realized he could back off a few degrees. Always best to make things easy. He walked to the far side of his desk and pressed a button on his phone. "Mary-Beth, bring Ben a glass of water would you?"

He set the phone down and studied the boy in silence. A moment later Mary-Beth presented a tumbler of water and closed the door as she left.

Ben took a long drink and tried to imagine what he could say. He decided to start with a question of his own. "What makes you think I know anything about this gun?"

Gruman tried to smile. "Let me provide you with its most recent history. Last night Donnel Smeardon was pulled from the ocean. Drowned. Did you know that?"

Ben glanced away. "Yes."

"I'm sure you did." He walked beside the desk. "Your father's pistol, the one in front of you now, was found on his body, tucked under his belt. Did you know that?"

"Dad told me." Ben looked at the sheriff. For the first time he could keep his eyes on him.

"Yes, but your dad denied that he gave the gun to Smeardon." He continued to stare at the boy. "I'd like you to tell me who you think gave Smeardon that pistol."

Ben opened his mouth to speak and looked away. He wet his lips and said, "I did."

"*You* did."

"Yessir." With this confession out of the way, he suddenly felt that the worst of his culpability was now on record. If he'd committed any crime, that was the extent of it. The only thing that remained was to demonstrate that he'd had nothing to do with Smeardon taking drugs from Jackie Spitzer. And absolutely nothing to do with Smeardon's drowning.

"And you gave it to him for … money?"

"No."

"Drugs?"

"No!"

Gruman held a hand over his mouth. "You gave it to him because you wanted to be cool?"

Ben thought for a moment. This was the closest he could get to an actual reason. "Something like that."

The sheriff stared at him and let out a long sigh of disbelief. "All right. When did you last see him?"

"On Monday. On the way to school."

"I understood that Donnel hasn't attended class for two weeks."

He shrugged. "I don't know. I was on my way to school. He was on his bike. I flagged him down and asked for the gun. I told him Dad would find out it was missing."

Gruman wondered about the look on Ben's face. Confessional, contrite, remorseful. If he could feel sorry for the boy, now would be the time to tell him. "All right. I believe you. Can you tell me why Smeardon wanted the gun in the first place?"

"He said he wanted to take it to a drug deal. But he only told me that *after* I gave it to him." Ben shook his head. Did this implicate him in another crime? Conspiracy of some kind? He pressed the balls of his hands to his eyes and pushed back the tears.

"What drug deal?"

"I don't know." He looked into the sheriff's face. "I honestly don't know. I don't know anything more. *Fuck.*"

Gruman rolled his upper lip over the lower and realized there was no more juice to squeeze from the boy. The best he could do would be to leave him with a warning. Put the fear into him. "Ben, how close do you think you are right now to being charged with a felony?"

Ben lifted his hands, let them drop in his lap. "I don't know."

Gruman sat on the edge of the desk again. He stared down into the boy's face. "This close." He held his thumb and index finger a quarter inch apart. "Now what do you think is holding me back from charging you right now with two, maybe three criminal charges?

"I don't know, sir." Ben took another sip of water.

"Me." Gruman raised his eyebrows.

"I don't understand."

"You don't *understand?!*" He leaned forward. *"Me.* I'm the only person in this world standing between you and the fucking slammer. *Now do you get that?"*

"Yessir," Ben whispered. "I get it."

※

Three hours later Ben lay on his bed staring at a poster of LeBron James taped to the ceiling above his head. He drifted in and out of the funk that had squeezed him in its grip over the past week. Every time he thought that he might be nearing the end of this misery, a new phantom would emerge. The latest being the threat of arrest for a criminal felony. Worse, the decision to arrest him could be triggered by a mere whim. And apart from a statute of limitations — what, ten years? — Gruman's threat had no limit. The sheriff could pull him aside five,

171

seven, nine years from now and throw him in jail on the spot. Insane. That's what his life had become in just two weeks. *Deranged.*

He tapped the screen of Donnel Smeardon's iPhone 6. Even though it had no data or telephone service, the wireless connection worked flawlessly and the phone was loaded with a ton of apps, videos, music, games. He could never tell his parents he'd swapped this for the Glock; in fact, it seemed dangerous just to hold it in his hand. But he could get so lost in its digital labyrinth, wander mindlessly for hours from porn to military games to brain-numbing clips on YouTube. A complete and perfect distraction from the world. Only two of his friends owned one of these and he could see why everyone lusted after them. He wondered who owned the iPhone before it came into Donnel's possession. But no matter who might be its rightful owner, he realized that he should turn it over to his father. With that surrender would come a final confession, hopefully the last time he'd have to come clean about his brief encounters with Donnel Smeardon.

As he clicked from screen to screen another twenty minutes passed before he stumbled upon a file named *0427.mp3.* He tapped the screen icon. A moment passed in which he could hear a grating sound through the earpiece, as if fabric or clothing was rubbing against a microphone. He boosted the volume and heard the sound of two men talking in low tones. He sat up on the bed and narrowed his eyes. Who were they? Donnel. Yes, he could make out Donnel's nasal whine, his slang, his mumbling expressions. The other voice was flat, and then it rose with bleak authority. Could it be? Sheriff Gruman.

CHAPTER FOURTEEN

"WALLY, I REALLY think I need to wrap this up." Will Finch stared at the beige paint on the motel wall and wondered how he'd endured five nights in room 203.

He switched his cell phone from his right ear to his left. The conversation with Wally Gimbel had gone longer than he'd imagined it would. He had intended to check in, let Wally know that he'd ferreted out as much of the story in Astoria as he could. The rest he could handle on the phone from his desk back at the *eXpress*. His one week on location had been profitable, no doubt. In fact he expected the story of Ray Toeplitz's murder to blow wide open once Jennie Lee launched a formal investigation. But the question pivoted on when she'd get to it. He explained how the local politics had slowed the investigation to a crawl. Furthermore, he couldn't release the statement against the Whitelaw boys from Gianna until he obtained corroborating testimony from someone else. Wally agreed. The story was just too explosive. Besides, the twins would argue that their half-sister had an interest in humiliating the family because they'd turned her lover away. Even more troubling was Jennie's last call and her claim that the chain of evidence pointing to the Whitelaws had broken. Perhaps Donnel Smeardon, an eighteen-year-old drug dealer and school dropout, had shot Toeplitz. The fact that Smeardon himself had drowned within a week of the murder seemed much too convenient, but how could Finch pursue that line of inquiry? No matter what happened now, Finch knew the story angle had switched from "California Kennedys are Killers" to "Dime-bag Dealer Delivers Death."

"You know what Patch Simpson used to tell me when my stories dried up?" Wally sounded nostalgic. Once a year or so, he'd refer to his deceased mentor, the revered editor at the *San Francisco Herald.*

"Patch Simpson?" Finch rolled his eyes. "What'd he say?"

"Throw some water on it. And if that doesn't work, throw on some gasoline. Then wait for someone to light a match."

"Not bad." Finch tried to force a laugh. His mind turned to Gianna. "But seriously, I think I'm going to get an early night tonight and drive back tomorrow. Did you know it takes twelve hours to drive home from here?"

"It's your call." Wally's voice lowered to a more serious tone. "But if things do break between now and tomorrow morning, stick with it up there. The stories you've filed so far are getting a lot of attention. The first person piece about the bear necropsy has been picked up across the country and into Europe."

"Europe, too?"

"Yeah. And down-under. They're eating it up." He laughed again. "Sorry, I couldn't help that."

Finch cringed. Wally didn't usually serve up puns peppered

with black humor. Will was about to comment when he heard a tap at the door. With the phone still at his ear, he walked to the entry and cracked it open. The look on the face standing before him made him pause.

"Wally I've got to go," he said. "Something's just come up."

※

"Ben, what happened?" Will Finch was struck by the grimace of exhaustion on the boy's face as he stood at the door. What he saw puzzled him, then his confusion turned to concern. "Jeez, come on in. Are you all right?"

Ben Argyle took a few steps into the room. Finch scanned the motel walkway — an outdoor, open-air balcony — and then closed the door behind him. He stepped past Ben and then turned to face him. The young man's posture curved at the shoulders, his sweater skipped a button above his belly, his cheek fuzz covered a rash of acne.

"Sit down, Ben." He pulled the chair away from the laminate desk so that it faced the bed. "Let me take your jacket."

Ben slipped his school jacket from his shoulders and slumped into the chair. He glanced about the room. "This is what you get for $49.95 a night?"

Finch smiled and tossed the jacket onto the dresser opposite the bed. "There's a bathroom, too." He crooked his thumb towards the door. "And it comes with maid service. Sometimes daily."

The corners of Ben's mouth slid into an amused frown. He was glad to hear a note of cynicism in Finch's voice. He studied him carefully, tried to determine if he could trust him.

175

"Wow. That's a close look you're giving me," Finch said when he realized he was being sized up.

Ben shrugged as if looks didn't count for a damn.

"…So…." Finch paused and then continued, "I'm not sure what brought you here. I'm going to guess that something's come up. Something big enough that you can't talk about it with anyone else in Astoria."

Ben blinked, a sign that Finch took as an affirmation.

"And the reason everyone in Astoria is disqualified is because this thing, whatever it is, *is about Astoria.*" He raised his eyebrows. "Am I right?"

"Sort of." He sniffed, ran an index finger under his nostrils.

"Okay." Finch wondered how to drag the story out of the boy. Time to be blunt about it. "Ben, do you want me to *guess* what happened?"

Ben took a long breath and shrugged again. Then he drew the iPhone from his pocket. "This belonged to Donnel Smeardon," he said.

"The kid who drowned and then turned up on the wharf last night?"

"After we left Saddle Mountain, you said I could contact you if anything else came up. Does that still stand?"

Finch leaned forward. "Of course."

"Okay, so something's come up." He looked away, then turned his head back to Finch. "But it's *seriously* bad." He pursed his lips. "I'm worried."

"And it's on this phone?" Finch pointed to the iPhone but did not touch it.

"Mm-hm."

"And is the phone itself evidence of some kind?"

"What's on it is."

"And who knows about it?"

He shook his head. "Just you and me."

"All right." Finch leaned back and wondered how to proceed. "So what is it?"

Ben turned his mouth, felt the tendons crunch in his jaw. He'd thought about this moment, the time when he'd reveal to someone what had happened to Smeardon. He'd decided then that he'd have to go forward. He reaffirmed that now when he realized that the only person who could assemble the pieces of this crazy puzzle was Will Finch.

"It's an audio file I found — a voice recording of Donnel Smeardon and Sheriff Gruman. It's the two of them talking, from what I think is the inside of the sheriff's squad car. I'm sure Donnel recorded it as he was being busted for dealing pot a few days after I loaned him my father's Glock."

Finch held a hand up to stop him from saying another word. "Wait a second. *Your father's Glock?*"

Ben closed his eyes and nodded.

"Was it a nine millimeter?"

"Yes."

Exactly what Jennie Lee had claimed. Finch glanced away, then turned back to the boy. "Okay, so tell me again, how did Smeardon get your father's pistol?"

Ben closed his eyes a moment. "I gave it to him."

"You did?"

"Mm-hm." He held Finch's eyes and continued. "Dad already knows about it. So does the sheriff."

Finch took a moment and tried to assemble the facts. "How did they find out?

Ben described the interrogations he'd endured with his father and Gruman. The more he talked, the more his voice settled and he accepted all that had happened including the role he'd played in putting the pistol into Smeardon's hands. "It's my fault," he concluded, "and I accept it."

Finch nodded when the boy finished his confession. That, and the fact that he was here to reveal something new about the pistol earned Finch's respect. "All right. Can we listen to this file now?"

"Just tap the file and hit the play button."

"I can't. Because of the forensics, the only person who can touch that phone from now on is you."

※

"The fuck are you doing?"

"Careful, that's a language violation, Smeardon." Gruman's voice sounded charitable. Relaxed. "But since you ask so nicely," he continued, "I'm busting you."

"For what? I done nothing wrong, man."

"Let's see now." Gruman's voice rose a note, as if he'd heard this question a hundred times from various drug felons, and each time he was granted an opportunity to begin a new round of manipulations. "How about possession of a controlled substance for starters? Empty your pockets and we'll see if I can limit this to simple possession."

"Possession?"

"Instead of more serious options."

"What's *more* serious?"

178

"If your cargo tips the scales, then it becomes possession for the purpose of trafficking. And believe me, you don't want to see this quiet social gathering of ours go in that direction."

After a brief silence Donnel sighed, a sound Finch almost mistook for a moan. Then he could hear the sounds of clothing shuffling, a zipper tugged, snagged and pulled free.

"Put it all on the dashboard, Smeardon."

More sighs.

"All right. Stop there." Gruman's voice shifted to a low throttle. "What's that in your jacket pocket?"

"Nothing. Just my personal stuff."

"On the dashboard. Now."

"What if I tell you, no way?"

"What if I tell you that in ten minutes Biff Winslow is going to strip search you in the privacy of one of our sound-proof jail cells?"

"Fuck!"

"Careful what you ask for, Smeardon."

This time the moan from Donnel Smeardon sounded like a cry of pain. "All right," he said. "You don't need to hit me."

"Hit you? When I hit you, you won't be able to complain. Now get it on the dashboard."

"All right."

"Jesus...." Gruman paused as if he had to consider how to proceed. "A nine-millimeter Glock. Now how did this little nightmare come into your possession, Smeardon?"

"Look, I never fired that thing. Not a shot."

"That demonstrates good character on your part, Smeardon, but that's not what I asked."

"I just had to use it for show. That's all. I swear I never pulled the trigger on that thing."

"Just for show, huh? And that's how you managed to boost Jackie Spitzer's marijuana grow-op. Is that right?"

A moment of silence broke the conversation. A recording glitch?

"You know, Donnel, you should not be messing with Jackie." Gruman's voice sounded even, rational, layered with benevolence. "If you show up dead one day, the first person I'll suspect will be Jackie Spitzer. Hell, everyone in the county will be happy to see that bastard put away. And if it's because he popped a dime slug through your head, then we'll all appreciate your assistance in our investigation of him and I promise to mention that at your memorial service. Now, if that sounds like a future career track to you then — "

The recording cut in and out, then resumed.

"Get out of the car and consider yourself lucky."

A few seconds of static muffled the dialogue.

"I want the Glock back — "

"Unless you tell me where you got it, you will never see this gun again." Gruman in the distance. Had Smeardon climbed out of the squad car?

"I'm serious."

"Me too, Donnel. Me too." As the recording faded, Finch could almost hear the sound of Gruman's scowl crawling across the sheriff's face.

※

Finch ran a hand under his jaw and stared at the wall. He'd never heard more vital incriminating evidence revealed in a voice recording. The fact that Gruman took possession of the pistol used to murder Toeplitz, and that the same gun appeared on Smeardon's corpse … meant what?

He turned his head to Ben and tried to read the boy's face. He looked calm now, relieved to have shared the iPhone recording with someone else. "Are there any more recordings on the phone?"

"I couldn't find any."

Who could tell? The phone would have to be processed by an expert. Finch stood up and paced along the foot of the bed and turned back to Ben.

"Ben, I'm convinced this phone is important physical evidence in a crime."

"You mean about Donnel?"

"Donnel and something much bigger."

"What?" A look of fear crossed his face.

"There's no need to panic, but your fingerprints are all over that cell. With any luck, there will be more evidence like that recording to tie it to Donnel, too. In the meantime, I encourage you not to touch the phone again, except for one more time. After that, I urge you to seal it in a plastic bag and turn it over to the local authorities."

Ben began to speak but choked on the words in his throat. He coughed and then continued. "You mean give it to the sheriff?"

"No. If I were you, I'd give it to the county medical examiner, Jennie Lee. She knows the background. Believe me, she can protect you."

"Protect me? Why do *I* need protection?" Ben looked up

from the chair as a wave of fear washed through him.

"You only need protection as long as you, and *only* you, hold onto that phone and as long as that recording is the only copy available. Think about it. What if Gruman discovers the evidence in your hands?" Finch stood before the boy and tried to deflect some of the fear he could see in his face. "I want you to consider a plan. I want you to email that file to my phone. Once I have it, I'll copy it to my computer and upload it to the *SF eXpress* server. Our network is completely secure, I guarantee you."

He paused to ensure that Ben was following. The boy nodded and Finch continued.

"It's almost certain Gruman has no idea this phone or the recording even exists. If he did, he'd turn day into night looking for it. But once the file is copied and transferred, the best way to guarantee your safety is if I tell Sheriff Gruman that I've sent the recording to my office. I will not mention your name and I will never reveal to him that you are my source. When he understands this, any threat to you will be minimized. In other words the cat will be out of the bag, but no one will know who released it, or how to herd it back into hiding."

He nodded. "All right. But how will Gruman find all this out?"

Finch crossed his arms over his chest and tried to relax. "Once I have the recording on my phone, I'll pay him a visit. Tonight. I'll play the conversation back to him. As a journalist I'll ask him if he has any opinion on it."

A look of surprise crossed Ben's face. "You will?"

Finch nodded. "That's how I do my job."

The boy glanced across the room. Can you just do that? He turned back to Finch. "All right. I'll do it. But I don't have a data plan for the phone."

"The Prest has free wireless. One more perk for my $49.95. Here's the password."

Finch gave Ben the password card presented to him by the motel receptionist. Ben entered it into the iPhone and a moment later the file buzzed into Finch's cell phone. He sent the recording to his laptop, opened the mail program and transferred the data from the laptop to the *eXpress* server. He figured that the three-step pass would ensure that no one could back-trace the file any further from the *eXpress* to his own phone. If the data nerds from the FBI got involved, he could "lose" his phone to ensure there'd be no link to Ben. Hopefully an unnecessary precaution.

With the digital file transfers complete, Finch passed Ben a plastic bag from his courier satchel. "Now, give the iPhone to Dr. Lee. She's over in the Medical Examiner's office. Do you know where that is?"

He nodded.

"And tell her I want her to keep it secured and in confidence. I'll phone to tell her you're coming."

"Right now?"

"Believe me, you want to get that out of your hands and into Dr. Lee's ASAP. And don't worry, she'll be working late." He considered the plan and then added, "I want you to play the file for her, too. Make sure she hears it. She's on our side."

"Okay." Ben stood up and took his jacket in his free hand. "But first tell me what crime you were talking about. Besides

Donnel, I mean."

Finch shook his head. He'd almost forgotten. His first reaction was to keep all the information he had confidential. Then he considered how the story would break out. This new evidence was explosive. An hour ago all his leads had turned to dust; he was ready to pack his bag and drive back to San Francisco. Wally would say that Ben had provided the water he needed to nurse the story back to life. At the very least, Finch owed Ben the truth.

"All right," he began. "You deserve to know. But I want you to pledge not to reveal what I'm going to tell you until I give you permission." Finch raised his eyebrows with a look of expectation.

He nodded. "I promise."

"It all starts with the bear you and your father stumbled across last weekend. What you didn't know is that the driver of that Mercedes was murdered before the bear found him. Shot twice with your father's nine-millimeter Glock."

CHAPTER FIFTEEN

JENNIE LEE SAT at her desk in the office adjacent to the pit and tried to put the events of the past few days in perspective. Will Finch had drawn the only logical conclusion based on the evidence at hand: Toeplitz had been murdered before the bear came across his corpse. The murder weapon had been identified and matched to the pistol found on the body of Donnel Smeardon. But what possible motive could he have had for shooting Toeplitz? Furthermore, did he have the guts for this kind of crime? According to Biff Winslow, Smeardon had spent a few months in juvenile detention. The probability that this kid could jump from misguided youth to killer-for-hire was pretty low. But, she had to admit, it does happen.

When her cell phone buzzed she read Finch's name on the screen. Every time he called, she heard one more demand from him. Or rather, a polite request offered in the form of a bargain, an information-sharing partnership of some kind. Reporters. The finagling they had to do.

She hesitated, then decided to answer. Maybe he had a new piece to add to the puzzle.

"I want you to know that I almost didn't pick up."

Finch paused, tried to decode this statement, and then pressed on. "Look, I just sent Ben Argyle to find you. He's got Donnel Smeardon's iPhone. The phone contains an audio recording of him speaking to Sheriff Gruman."

Jennie leaned forward in her chair. "All right. You've got my attention. What's on the recording?"

"Ask Ben to play it for you. In one sentence, it proves Gruman had the Glock in his possession before Toeplitz was shot. I don't have time to say more. I'm going straight up to Gruman's place. Just secure the iPhone when Ben gives it to you and don't let Gruman know you have it."

"What?"

"I'll check in with you when I get back."

After he hung up, Jennie stared at her phone. A sense of foreboding crawled through her stomach. Did Finch know what he might be getting into?

A moment later she heard someone walking along the basement hallway toward her office. She shuddered when she imagined it might be Gruman himself. A tap at the door, and Biff Winslow poked his head through the opening.

"You still here?"

She shrugged and examined the deputy sheriff. An old friend of Gruman's, she'd never felt she could trust him. The two of them, and many others around town, played the old-boy network like a team sport. The only thing they needed was matching baseball caps. Besides, she simply didn't like the look of Winslow: a bag of soggy meat and bones and a look in his eyes that detected conspiracy everywhere.

"Why would I leave?" she said. "Today just gets weirder

with every passing hour."

Winslow pasted a smile on his face and pulled at the chin hairs of his goatee. "Brace yourself, I think it's about to get weirder."

"Why's that?" Jennie tipped her head toward the empty chair.

Winslow sat down and set a photograph on her desk. "Do you recognize that?"

She took the photo in her hand. "It's a fish trap of some kind. A shrimp trap?"

Winslow studied her. He knew she was bright enough — a doctor, after all — but could he trust her? "It's a prawn trap, same thing really. The one pulled onto the *Osprey Nest* with Donnel Smeardon last night."

"Right. I remember it now. This picture was taken on the deck of the boat by the forensic photographer."

Winslow nodded. "And what else do you see there?"

Jennie narrowed her eyes. Why did she have to answer all these questions? She set the photograph back on the desk. "Biff, is there something you want to tell me about the prawn trap?"

He nodded his head and thought a moment. He wanted her to see what lay before her eyes. That way, he wouldn't bear any responsibility. He leaned forward. "I could lose my job for this. Or worse."

Jennie leaned back in her chair. She'd never seen so much group paranoia. "Look, I've been working here for almost a year now and it's taken me that long to realize that every third person speaks in code. Or some kind of special dialect designed to skirt around the county gestapo. Now please, tell me. What is going on?"

He nodded. At least she got it. "I need to know I can trust you."

She smiled. "That's funny, you know, because I don't know that *I* can trust *you*."

He lowered his eyes and looked at his hands. It would be easier to leave the room right now and forget about this entire conversation. And safer. He decided to plunge ahead.

"All right. Look at the discoloration in this picture." He pointed to a yellow badge attached to the trap frame.

Jennie took a close look, then held a small magnifying glass over the image. "It looks like a brand tag of some kind. Maybe a manufacturer's label."

"No. It's an owner's tag." The deputy's face began to relax. He was halfway into this now and he felt better about confiding in the doctor. "To get a license, every prawner is required to identify his traps."

"Really?" Jenny took a closer look at the image. "But can you make out someone's name on this?"

"No. But you can on this picture." He set a second photograph on her desk, a close-up of the brass ownership tag.

She looked at the image and turned her eyes to Winslow. "Mark Gruman," she whispered.

He nodded his head, a series of almost invisible motions, up and down.

"And this trap was tied to Donnel Smeardon's hand when he died. Am I right?"

Winslow sat in silence. He ran a hand over his face and

pulled at the end of his goatee again.

"Biff, tell me if Sheriff Gruman's prawn trap was tied to Donnel Smeardon's wrist!"

"Yes," he whispered. "It was."

Her heart jumped a beat and she paused to study him a moment. "Let me ask you a personal question. Why are you showing me these pictures? I thought you and Gruman were like this." She held up her hand, index and middle fingers pressed together.

"We go back, all right," the deputy said. "And Mark was a hero in the first Gulf war. Hell, that's why everyone votes for him. But this" — he shook his head and stared at the photographs — "it stretches beyond friendship. No matter how far back you go." His voice dropped a tone. "I think Mark killed that boy."

Jennie sighed and glanced away. "Jesus."

"I know," he said. "We have a serious problem on our hands."

※

When they heard more footsteps coming toward them along the hallway Jennie and Winslow cut their conversation. Once again Jennie thought it might be Gruman but then the steps hesitated, turned, walked away, then turned again. She glanced at Winslow and mouthed a question: *Do you know who it is?*

He shrugged, no.

Jennie's heart began to race. She slid the two photographs into a file folder and tucked them inside a desk drawer. With luck, Gruman would never know she'd seen the incriminating images.

"Dr. Lee?" A voice called softly from the corridor. "Is there a Dr. Lee down here?"

With a glance to the deputy she let out a sigh of relief.

"In here." Jennie rose from her chair and walked to the door. "You must be Ben Argyle?"

"Yes."

"Come on in." She led him into her office and pointed to her chair. When she saw the pallor of his face, the way the boy's head ticked nervously from side to side as he examined the office, she wanted to comfort him. "Take a seat, Ben," she said with a smile.

When he sat down she introduced him to Winslow and looked down at the boy.

"We've met," the deputy said. "Good to see you, Ben."

"Will Finch called to tell me you'd be coming by. Apparently you have something I'm to keep under lock and key." She smiled again.

Ben glanced at Winslow. A look of doubt crossed his face.

"It's okay," Jennie said in a reassuring tone. "We can all trust one another here, can't we, Mr. Winslow?"

"Yes," he said. Winslow realized he was in it with both feet now. Playing for the other team was his only hope for survival. "Yes, absolutely. Trust is all we have."

Jennie glanced from Biff to Ben. "Mr. Finch said you have a recording that I should listen to. Is that right?"

Ben nodded, hesitated a moment and then drew the iPhone from his pocket. He pulled it from the plastic baggie, set it on the table, turned it on and touched the audio file. "The file's sketchy in a few places, but you can still hear most of it."

CHAPTER SIXTEEN

WILL FINCH DROVE the Ford Tempo up the rutted gravel track toward Bob Wriggly's house. The mist had turned to a steady, thin rain and he was surprised to see Wriggly outside, working on a gatepost at the edge of his property. Finch pulled over and lowered his window.

"You must be getting pretty wet out here," he said and glanced at the shed housing Toeplitz's car. "Is the Mercedes still in the shop?"

"Liquid sunshine," Wriggly said and smiled. He set his tools aside and ambled toward the Ford Tempo. A narrow rivulet of rainwater slipped from the peak of his ball cap. "What brings you up this way?"

"I thought I'd pay a visit to the sheriff. He's up the hill, right?" Finch pointed along the gravel track.

Bob Wriggly frowned and brushed a hand over his face. "It's the only place up there. A hand-made geodesic dome set back a hundred yards from the edge of the road. Nobody knows where he came up with the idea. Leaks like a perforated tin can, too." He smiled, a look of amusement. "What's cooking up there?"

Finch took in the old man's congeniality. If he managed to live into his sixties Finch hoped that he might develop something resembling Wriggly's attitude. "I just thought the sheriff might help me tie up a few loose ends on the story before I head back to San Francisco." He crooked a thumb to Wriggly's workshop. "Speaking of which, what's become of Toeplitz's car?"

Wriggly shrugged. "Not a word from anyone since you were here. Still sits in its cage like a glorious black raven," he said and smiled.

Finch shook his head and glanced up the hill. Obviously Jennie had either done nothing to press for a criminal investigation of Toeplitz's murder — or she'd tried and failed. Otherwise the Mercedes would be impounded by now.

"If that changes, be sure to call or email me, would you?"

"You bet," he said. "I've got your card."

Finch smiled at him. "You're a good man, Bob. I don't know how you do it."

"It's my home-made granola, I guess." He laughed and showed his discolored teeth.

"Send me the recipe, would you?" Finch laughed and drove on to the top of the hill.

※

After they listened to the recording, Jennie clicked off the iPhone and pushed it toward Deputy Winslow with her gloved hand.

"Mr. Finch was smart to advise you to bring this in," she said to Ben, then glanced at the deputy for confirmation.

"She's right. I know this has been hard on you, but you've

done everything required by the law. And common decency," Winslow added. "I'll keep the phone locked in the evidence room. If there's nothing else you want to add, then I need to speak to Dr. Lee in private."

Ben nodded, and as if he needed another moment to digest the deputy's meaning, he paused and then rose from the chair.

"One more thing." Jennie held a hand in the air. "This took a lot of guts on your part. But look, if Sheriff Gruman wants to talk to you or see you, I want you to say no. Then I want you to call Deputy Winslow here, or me. Do not meet with him and do not speak to him. Do you understand me?"

She gave him her card and he nodded as he gazed at the embossed lettering on the card.

"All right. Now do you need a drive back home?" She glanced at Winslow, a gesture that assigned the task to him.

"No, I've got my bike."

"Okay, then I want you to call me when you get there. How long does it take to pedal home?"

"Ten minutes."

"All right." Winslow smiled with a stern look that carried a hint of affection. "If you haven't called Dr. Lee within fifteen minutes, I'm gonna come and find you. Got that?"

"Yes sir."

"Thanks, Ben." Jennie led him down the basement corridor and watched a moment to ensure he closed the door. Then she locked it.

When she returned to her office, Biff Winslow stood at the wall, his fists bunched on his hips as he studied a laminated poster that revealed a cut-away view of the human anatomy.

"Too bad you don't have a chart showing the details of the psychopathic mind," he mused.

"Yeah, I guess we could use that. Maybe it would tell us something about the real Mark Gruman. And about how many people he's killed."

Winslow let out a laugh. "We could use a lot more than that," he said and turned to face her. "With the iPhone recording, the slugs matched to the Glock, and the name plate on the prawn trap, all the physical evidence points to Gruman. We're going to have to bring him in."

"In that case, better do it soon. Will Finch has just gone out to Gruman's home to confront him."

"What?"

She nodded and examined his eyes, saw the growing dread in his face.

"I'm going to have to call in some help," he said as if he felt an enormous weight pressing on his chest. "This is growing into one hell of a mess."

※

At first Mark Gruman felt a tinge of surprise when he spotted Will Finch driving up the gravel track to his home. For the past three years, after word had spread through the county that he'd installed surveillance monitors around his property, he rarely had any spontaneous visitors. Pop-ins, he used to call them. Finch might pop in unannounced, he mused, but who could say how he'd leave?

He walked to a sectioned-off side of the dome he'd designed as his office space and unlocked the cabinet which he'd bolted to the wall. He studied the contents a moment and drew out the Smith & Wesson HP64 and ensured it was loaded. He moved back to the living room, opened the drawer in the coffee table, slid the pistol under a magazine and walked back to the surveillance monitor. He could see Finch ease out of his car, hunch his shoulders against the rain and make his way up the trail to the front door of the dome.

He turned off the monitor and strolled into the living room, switched on the TV and clicked over to the Sports Channel. The Seattle Mariners versus the Toronto Blue Jays, bottom of the eighth, Jays leading seven to three. He decided the best approach to Finch would be to play a game of *surprise me*. Let Finch take the lead, say what he might, lay down his cards — and then gasp in shock at his little fantasy. Journalists. Fucking leeches.

He didn't answer the first knock, but after a brief pause Gruman padded silently to his front door and swung it open. He caught Finch glancing back at his car. The surprise now belonged to him.

"Well, well. Look what the wind blew into my yard."

Finch turned and looked into the sheriff's eyes. "So you are here."

"Oh I'm here, all right." A weak smile fluttered on his lips. "And what drags you up to this end of the world?"

Finch peered past Gruman into the house. He flicked his jacket collar and the rain fell along his neck. "May I come in?"

"Depends on what you're selling."

"I'm not selling anything. I'm giving you the chance to go on record about the murder of Raymond Toeplitz."

Gruman took a backward step and then leaned forward.

"For the record," he said as his voice hardened, "there *was* no murder of Raymond Toeplitz."

"That's not what the evidence shows." Will narrowed his eyes and locked them on Gruman. "Now can I come in to discuss this, or should I print the conversation you had with Donnel Smeardon and let the unedited transcript stand without your version of the facts?"

Gruman nudged his jaw forward and set his teeth. What is he talking about?... *Could it be?*... Another moment passed before he made his decision. "All right. Besides, I'm in no mood to watch the Mariners lose to the fucking Jays." He swung a hand into the room and closed the door behind Finch.

Will took a few steps into the dome and examined the room. Gruman had patched together a geodesic dome based on the models of Buckminster Fuller. Some sections were made of glass and provided views into the front yard, others looked onto the forest that stood a few feet behind the farthest wall. The curving walls appeared to be constructed from scrap wood panels and fiberboard, and then filled with rough, unpainted plaster. The round ceiling was a patch-work too, and he could see five or six areas discolored by dampness. A mismatched collection of furniture divided the living space into two areas: a living room, where the TV flashed a replay of another run by the Toronto Blue Jays, and a kitchen that included a small table, refrigerator, electric stove and sink. Three free-standing walls, which stopped a good six feet below the cavernous ceiling, marked off areas that Finch assumed were a bedroom, bathroom and another room whose purpose eluded him. Finch could smell mold festering somewhere under the rot. If anything, Bob Wriggly had underestimated the water damage soaked up by the house over the past few years.

Gruman clicked off the TV, sat next to the coffee table and leaned over the magazine in the open drawer. He pointed to the chair facing the kitchen. As Finch settled into the chair, Gruman tapped his protruding lips with his index finger. Whatever "evidence" Finch had would have to be neutralized, he thought. There'd be a way to do it, there always was, but he had to let Finch show his hand before he could devise a plan.

"You've got five minutes," he announced, "after that I'm going to turn my attention back to the game." Then, thinking he should offer a distraction, he added, "By the way, can I get you a beer?"

"Not drinking right now." Finch decided to skip any niceties. He would simply put his phone on the coffee table, hit the play button and observe Gruman's reaction to the Smeardon recording. As he reached into his courier bag he felt a vibration. An in-coming text.

"Really? Now that's interesting, Finch." He paused and lit a cigarette. "Something we have in common. I like to keep a beer on hand for company like yourself, but personally, I haven't had a drop since the Gulf war. Well over twenty years. How 'bout you? You ever done any service?" He exhaled a column of smoke, certain that Finch would never have survived boot camp.

"Four years in Baghdad," he said and angled his head to catch Gruman's reaction. "Gulf II."

"Really?" His eyebrows arched upward. "What capacity?"

"Public Affairs," he lied.

D. F. Bailey

Gruman leaned forward an inch. A smile crossed his lips. "Office boy, huh?"

Finch glanced at his phone. A message from Jennie. He clicked on the message icon and studied the text: *Gruman killed Smeardon. We have proof.* He switched to the home screen and set the phone on the coffee table.

Now he felt an anxious distraction. What could her message imply? He paused to re-focus. "I'm not here to talk about me, Mark. This is about you and Smeardon." He leaned over and clicked on the audio file. Seconds later Smeardon's voice began to rise from the phone:

"The fuck are you doing?"

"Careful, that's a language violation, Smeardon.... But since you asked so nicely, I'm busting you."

As the audio file played out Finch watched Gruman's face, waited for him to signal that he'd heard enough.

But Gruman betrayed no emotion whatsoever, not a hint of surprise or anxiety. The moment he heard his voice rising over Smeardon's near-illiterate rants he realized that a serious problem had to be eliminated. But how? He decided to wait until the recording came to an end, determine the extent to which he might be incriminated, and use the time to formulate a plan. He thought of the Smith & Wesson hidden under the magazine. He had the firepower, no doubt, but not the advantage of time. He knew he had to stall and somehow move Finch out of the house. The question of due legal process could well be on his side, too. He decided to play that gambit first, and see where it led. When the voice recording concluded he stubbed out his cigarette in one of the ashtrays scattered across the table and shifted his gaze back to Finch.

"Tell me something, Finch. How did you come into possession of that tape?"

"I have my sources. This one is protected by reporter's privilege." Finch leaned over and clicked his phone to record his current conversation with Gruman. "So, we're on record now," he said and added the date, time and place of their interview. He realized that Gruman had failed to acknowledge that he'd begun to record their dialogue. No matter; he'd given him proper warning.

"There's no reporter's privilege if you came by that tape illegally."

Don't get caught up in the details, Will thought. "All right. The digital file of you in conversation with Donnel Smeardon came to me as a gift. There's nothing illegal about how I got it. The only issue I'm interested in now, is if you have a comment that you want to put on the record."

Gruman leaned back in the chair and lit another cigarette. "All right, Finch. What exactly are you accusing me of? Is there some *crime* that's been committed that I don't know about? And if there is, by the way, *you* have a legal obligation to inform me of it. And promptly, I might add."

Finch stiffened. "The crimes are the premeditated murders of Donnel Smeardon and Raymond Toeplitz."

Gruman's jaw hung open as he laughed in an abrupt snort. *"Murder?!* Are you still going on about that? You're just trying to screw me six ways to Sunday by printing that bullshit, Finch. Go ahead. Do it. Then I'll figure out how many millions I can sue you and your toilet-paper tabloid for. Everybody from here to China knows Toeplitz was eaten — devoured — by a black bear. Hell, I understand you sat in on the necropsy. I heard you even fainted. That right?"

Finch ignored this. Obviously Manfred couldn't restrain himself from disclosing the episode in the pit. After Gianna revealed that Gruman was monitoring his local activities, he assumed every move he made was reported to the sheriff.

"Why don't you tell me your bird-brained theory of the crime. I'm all ears." Gruman waved his hands behind his ears and formed his lips in a mad grin.

"All right, Mark, the theory runs something like this. On Saturday afternoon, the Whitelaw twins traveled with Toeplitz in two cars from their family lodge in Cannon Beach up the switchbacks below Saddle Mountain. Evan Whitelaw drove in the passenger seat beside Toeplitz in his Mercedes, which is now parked in Bob Wriggly's garage. Justin Whitelaw led the way in his BMW. Once they reached the place where you'd agreed to meet them, Justin stopped, turned his car and blocked Toeplitz's way. Justin got out of his car, walked toward Toeplitz, signaling him to roll down his window."

He paused to see what effect this was having on the sheriff. Nothing. He pushed on.

"But sometime before their appearance, you'd arrived on the scene. When the window was down you approached from behind the driver's side of the car. Evan got out of Toeplitz's Mercedes, ran with his brother to the BMW, and together they drove off. At that point you leveled Ethan Argyle's Glock at Toeplitz and from a distance of about five feet you shot him twice, killing him instantly. The pistol was the same weapon you'd confiscated from Donnel Smeardon a few days earlier. A tidy bit of luck that you could exploit. But back to Toeplitz. After you murdered him, just after you picked up the brass from the Glock, something unexpected happened — something you thought would make the crime simply disappear. But it didn't work out so well."

Gruman sat in silence, mulling over the possibilities. "The unexpected, is it? Every crime writer must love this part of the story, Finch. Carry on." He lit another cigarette and waved a hand.

Finch leaned forward and continued. "That's when the bear appeared, Mark. At first it caught you by surprise. Because your car was parked out of sight, up around the bend in the road, you had to make a dash to get out of his way. That bear was hungry after all. *He was starving.* Maybe it was the first time you ever experienced real panic.

"So, how would I know that?" Finch waited to see what effect this question had. "Because you drove away, a little more than a half-mile down the switchback, *before* you threw the brass shells from the Glock down the hill. You didn't think anyone would ever pick up the brass, did you? But I did, Mark. In fact, here's a picture of them."

Finch leaned over his phone, clicked on the photo gallery and selected one of the images of the nine-millimeter brass lying on the ground where he found it. "Under a microscope, you can spot some partial fingerprints. I wonder who they belong to, don't you?"

Gruman glanced at the photo and nodded. "Go on."

"When we did the necropsy, we found the matching slugs

in the bear guts. But you knew that, too, didn't you? One of your moles, Manfred I imagine, passed that critical piece of info along to you. Yes, that's when I fainted, Mark, when I realized how much trouble this might cause you." Finch wet his lips and leaned forward. Only now did he realize the depth of his own bitterness. Reel it in, he told himself. Stick to the facts.

"But today, when I heard that recording, all the pieces fell into place. You took the Glock from Donnel Smeardon. The same pistol used to kill Toeplitz. And while the best solution for the gun would've been to toss it from the Astoria-Megler Bridge, you worried that Donnel Smeardon might tell the truth: that *you* had Ethan Argyle's pistol the day Toeplitz was murdered. So you dumped the gun with Smeardon into the ocean knowing that if Smeardon surfaced he'd be holding the pistol that shot Toeplitz. You'd be able to pin everything on that poor kid."

Gruman's mind began to race. His face erupted in another snort of laughter. "This's the deepest crock of horse shit I've heard since I left the army. Why the fuck would I get myself involved in any of this?"

"Because the Whitelaws promised you the one thing you need. The one thing they have in limitless supply." Finch leaned closer, close enough to study the web of lines that extended from Gruman's eyes down his cheeks. "Money," he whispered.

Gruman scanned the ceiling. The sound of rain slapped against the roof. Soon the water would begin to drip from the ceiling to the floor in a dozen well-worn spots. He angled toward the coffee table and wondered how to steer Finch outside. He would have to move him outside and into his truck. He glanced through the windows. He couldn't make out anything in the wet gloom.

When Gruman failed to respond, Finch spread his legs under the coffee table and pointed at his cellphone. "By the way, you should be aware that a copy of that recording is stored on a secure server in San Francisco. Tonight I'll ask my editor to open it and transcribe it. Within an hour it'll be posted on the internet."

Gruman seemed to awaken from his torpor. "I suppose you imagine that gives you some protection. All neat and tidy. *Finicky Finch*. Was that your handle when you were a public affairs flack in Iraq?"

Finch raised his eyebrows and stared at the sheriff with a look of disbelief. Gruman had no idea about his actual mission in Bagdad. "*That's* your comment on your conversation with Donnel Smeardon?"

Gruman drew his lips together and pulled his legs from under the sofa. He felt ready now. Almost eager. But he still had time enough to play with the little bird. He measured the distance between him and Finch. No more than two feet. "Let me tell you what people *call me*. People who know me well, that is. Back in the Gulf, during Desert Storm in '91, the boys in the 24th Infantry Division used to call me Bone Maker."

Finch reclined against the back of the chair. "Bone Maker," he repeated with a hint of amusement.

"Don't laugh. I had a knack for turning elite troops from the Iraqi Republican Guard into bones. White, broken bones that to this day are littered in the desert. Enough bones to win a bronze star."

He crooked his thumb toward a four-by-five-inch box-frame fixed to the wall above the kitchen table. Inside the glass display case, Finch could make out some military regalia. Above the frame stood a brass plaque inscribed with two words: OS FECIT.

"Latin for bone maker," he said when he saw Finch's puzzled look. "You got one of those from your newspaper?"

At first Finch ignored this, then he decided to take it up. "We've got something called the Pulitzer Prize. I don't imagine I'll ever pin one to a wall, but this kind of story — where a corrupt cop is exposed for double murder — it could put me in the running."

Gruman's jaw tightened. "I think it's time you moved on, Finch."

"Fine." He tapped his phone again and slipped it into his pocket.

"Not with that, I'm afraid." As he stood, his left hand reached toward Finch and he waved his fingers. *Gimme.*

"Sorry," Finch stood up.

"Don't be." Gruman shoved aside the magazine covering the coffee table drawer and lifted the Smith & Wesson into his right hand. "Now, give me the phone."

A rush of adrenaline swept through Finch's arms and chest. His throat tightened. "Look," he managed to say, his voice choking, "this is ridicu — "

With a single jab of his arm, Gruman smashed the butt of his pistol into Finch's left cheek. As Finch faltered, Gruman braced him under his left arm and fished the cell phone from the reporter's pocket.

"You should be more careful, Mr. Finch. Resisting arrest is a criminal offense." He whipped the pistol across Finch's face. The blow opened a cut below his eye.

As the blood drizzled down to his mouth Finch could feel a tooth fall from his lips. He looked across the room and considered sprinting to the door. If only. His legs buckled and he slumped against Gruman's chest.

"You know Finch, you seem to have forgot the public affairs golden rule: Never bring a cell phone to a gun fight." He laughed at this, then shifted his hip under Finch and adjusted an arm across his shoulders. The sheriff tightened his grip on the Smith & Wesson and began to frog-march Finch toward the front door, one step at a time as they stumbled past the sofa, along the worn carpet and across the unfinished fir floorboards.

Finch tried to speak but could not. With one final effort he pulled away from Gruman but was tugged back into place. He could smell his own wet blood and the stench of Gruman's nicotine-stained shirt. His tongue swept over the space between his teeth. How many had he lost? One, two?...

The sheriff eased open the door and gazed at the smudge of rain falling through the black drape of night. He calculated the distance to his truck. Maybe thirty feet. He could tie Finch to the open truck bed, drive him into the hills, finish him off, bury him and roll his Ford Tempo into a ravine. Finch would simply disappear. Flit away in the storm like a broken bird.

He took a dozen steps forward and noticed a break in the darkness ahead. Twin spears of light penetrated the air, then two more, and then another set. Seconds later, three vehicles pulled into his yard and parked in a tight row that blocked the driveway.

※

"Mark, best just to let Finch loose." Biff Winslow drew his pistol and stood behind the cover of the open truck door. A moment later eight other people emerged from the second and third pick-ups and crouched behind the vehicles, pistols and rifles pointed at Gruman and Finch.

"Biff, is that you? I can't believe that's you." Gruman pressed his forearm above his brow and tried to shield his eyes from the glare of the headlights. "Biff, get over here and help me. I'm taking Finch in for assault and resisting arrest." He spat out a laugh of disbelief. "This shit tried to take me down, if you can believe it."

"Mark, drop your pistol. Let Finch loose, and we can sort this out down at the station," Winslow yelled into the gusting wind. "I've got the sworn-in deputies here including Bob Wriggly and Ethan Argyle."

"Argyle?" Gruman grimaced and considered what this could mean. There was still a chance he could talk his way out of this. "Let him go? Fuck, I just lassoed him." He yanked Finch to his chest and tried to think. "Listen up, Biff. I'm going to make my way over to my truck and drive past you boys." He tightened his free arm around Finch's chest and pressed the Smith & Wesson to Finch's ear.

Winslow watched as the two men staggered towards the F150. As Gruman dragged Finch across the yard, Finch could manage only one or two steps on his own. "Sorry, Mark, that's just not going to work. We're arresting you for the murders of Donnel Smeardon and Raymond Toeplitz."

Gruman grunted and pushed Finch ahead of him. He knew that if he could make it to the truck, he'd be home-free.

From his position hunched on the hood of his Wrangler, Ethan Argyle watched the two men stumbling through the swirling rain. He balanced the barrel of the AR-15 rifle in the palm of his left hand and took a sighting on the front tire of Gruman's truck. Just wait, he whispered to himself. You'll know when.

"Mark, I want you to stop right there!" Winslow called out. "Now I mean it!"

Gruman lurched forward and Finch slumped along the wall of his chest. Finch's jaw felt like it had been transformed into a massive, ringing bell. With each step his head reverberated in pain.

"Don't screw this up, Mark. *Now you just stop there!*"

When Gruman refused to halt, Biff Winslow waved a hand at the deputies behind him. A second later a barrage of a dozen shots flashed through the body of Gruman's F150. The bullets punctured three of the tires exposed to the deputies' line of sight. Ethan Argyle knew for certain that he'd taken out the front left tire where the pressure valve protruded above the steel rim.

"You wet fucks!" Gruman cried. "What the hell are you doing? One of you might hit me, for christ sakes!"

He stopped and turned towards the men and the bank of headlights. Part of him now realized that it was over, that he was finished. He pressed the pistol to Finch's ear again and shook his head in dismay. The rain washed over his face. Beyond the glare of light streaming toward him from the row of trucks, the dark of night enveloped them all. He could feel himself sinking in a well of dread, a deep porous hole that would drown him. You could die here, he told himself. Die, and be gone for good.

Finch felt Gruman's body shudder and then totter toward the cars once more. As they stumbled ahead, he felt himself slide along the sheriff's torso down to his hip. Then the ringing in his head became a flash of pain as Gruman fired his pistol at Finch's ear. His head lit on fire and he screamed as a second barrage of bullets flew above him. He crashed to the ground, taken down by the weight of Gruman's limp body as it slumped across Finch's arms and back. The shooting stopped as a volley of stray bullets ripped through the forest behind the geodesic dome.

Ethan Argyle set his gun aside, sure that one of the bullets that killed Gruman had been fired from his AR-15. He'd lined the shot up with objective care, with a rational disdain void of any human emotion that might interfere with the moment of fate assigned to his control. The bullet had penetrated Mark Gruman's skull just above his right eye and exploded through the center of his brain. The sheriff wouldn't have felt anything other than the blitz of lightning striking his skull. Which was more than Ethan Argyle could say for every soul that Gruman had crushed or destroyed during his forty-seven years in this troubled world.

CHAPTER SEVENTEEN

As the ambulance coursed through the rain-drenched roads into town, Finch kept a wary eye on Gruman's corpse lying on the stretcher beside him. Despite the searing pain that radiated from his ear over the side of his head, Finch turned once or twice to ensure that Gruman couldn't lift himself and reach across the van to throttle him. Finally convinced that Gruman was dead, Finch swept an arm over the sheriff's corpse until his hand found the cellphone. He wrapped his fingers around his phone, guided it into his jacket pocket, and pulled the zipper tight. Now, he thought. Now I have it all.

The Columbia Memorial Hospital was more modern and efficient than Finch had imagined. The on-call physician did a quick assessment within minutes of Finch's arrival in the emergency ward. "It's your lucky day," he said. "That's the neatest bit of earlobe surgery I've seen in some time. The bullet cut off a little flesh on the lobule and the heat of the lead cauterized the wound. We'll just have to keep it clean to ensure there's no infection. Apart from that, I want to know if you have any hearing loss." He paused to determine if Finch had followed him so far. "Can you hear what I'm saying?"

Finch looked up at him, still in a daze. "Yeah, but my ear is ringing like I'm inside a church bell."

"Understandable. The paramedics said that the pistol was fired at the side of your head. I'll get an audiologist to do a complete assessment. Now let me examine your jaw and teeth."

When the doctor prodded the gum line, Finch screamed and almost jumped off the bed.

"This should help." He applied a dollop of analgesic to the root. The relief was immediate. "Your second molar on the upper left is broken from the root. Fortunately, the ambulance attendant recovered the tooth." He added that a dentist would bond the tooth to the root within the next hour. After Finch returned to San Francisco he'd need a local dentist to ensure no infection had set in. "When it's convenient."

"Convenient?" Finch said and he eased his head onto the pillow that the doctor fluffed up at the back of the bed.

"I'll give you some medication for the pain and some topical disinfectant to apply to your ear. Now turn your head to the side and I'll suture your cheek — probably just a stitch or two, enough to give you the look of a wounded hero. Tomorrow you'll be good to go."

The words made Finch wonder about his entire week in Astoria. On Monday, he'd never heard of the place. Now he was a patient in the local hospital, being treated for injuries inflicted by the recently deceased sheriff. If I'm good to go, he muttered, it'll be as far away from here as possible.

❊

"You were very lucky, Finch." Jennie Lee sat at the side of his hospital bed and shook her head with a look that expressed both envy and astonishment. "I really have to question your judgement, though. I mean, *what part of you* thought it was smart to confront Gruman on your own?"

Finch gazed at her face. Biff Winslow and the county prosecutor had just departed after an hour-long interrogation about the events leading up to Gruman's death. He felt exhausted from the ordeal and wanted nothing more than sleep.

"Finch?" She hesitated. "Are you with me?"

He blinked and forced himself to sit up. After a moment he said, "Biff Winslow just told me you were there last night. Is that right?"

She nodded. "He wanted someone other than the deputies to be able to testify to the facts. Smart move, as it turns out. With Gruman dead, there'll be a massive legal case to sort through. Hopefully it'll bring out whatever there is to learn about the Toeplitz and Smeardon murders."

Finch nodded, not so sure that an inquiry would prove much at all. The key players were dead, and the dead usually refuse to testify.

"There're other worries too. The state forensics team is already ramping up an investigation into the shootout last night. The deputies had to surrender their weapons and there'll be a match-up to determine who exactly shot the bullet that killed Gruman. Some people are calling it a firing-squad execution." She paused and glanced away.

"Not that it matters," she continued. "Ethan Argyle has already come forward. Said that he knows he fired the kill shot. From what Manfred and I determined this morning in the examining room, a 6.5mm Grendel was the only bullet to strike Gruman and Argyle was the only 6.5mm shooter. If that's all true, despite the circumstances, Argyle could very easily do some time in prison. You don't shoot a sheriff anywhere in this country without being put away to think twice about it."

Finch held a hand to his cheek and nodded. Bob Marley's reggae tune spun through his mind: *I Shot the Sheriff.*

"You know what's more bizarre? After Gruman fired his gun at your head, the deputies let off at least fifty rounds. But not one other shot hit Gruman. Not one. That tells me one of two things: they're either the worst shots this side of Canada, or none of them were willing to take Gruman down. Except for Ethan, every one of them remained loyal to Gruman."

"But not loyal enough to put a bullet in me," he muttered.

"Maybe they just wanted to bring him down a notch. Maybe they couldn't take his bullying any more."

Finch thought about this, about Jennie's version of the events that still flooded through his mind. He rolled his tongue over his newly bonded tooth. He tried to muster a comment, an observation, but all he could say was, "I'm glad you were there."

"Me too." She pulled herself up from the bedside chair and clutched her bag with both hands. "Looks like you need some sleep. I'll check in tomorrow." She leaned over and kissed him on the forehead. It was a motherly peck, a kiss without heat.

As Jennie walked out the door, Finch realized that it was time to go home. Once he had his medical discharge, he'd drive back to San Francisco and file two or three new stories on Ray Toeplitz's strange passing from the world. Maybe that would help him understand the growing list of questions at the back of his mind.

Alone at last, he pulled his phone from the night table and checked his messages. He scrolled through the index of texts and stopped on something new, a note from Gianna.

"Call me when you get in. I'm making dessert for two. Do you like chocolate mousse?"

CHAPTER EIGHTEEN

WALLY GIMBEL TRIED to be patient, but when he realized that Will seemed unable to grasp his point, he suspected that Finch's head injury had diminished the reporter's judgement. He adjusted the phone at his ear and attempted to clarify how they were going to proceed.

"Will, I agree that the overall story is yours. But you have to see it from an editorial perspective," he said. "And yes, you can write the story related to Toeplitz's murder. And the tragedy with the boy. But not the shoot-out with the sheriff. I'm giving that to Fiona Page. She's going to interview you and write the article for the simple reason that once Gruman dragged you onto his front yard and held a gun to your head, *you became the story.* Everything up to that point is yours. After that, it belongs to Fiona. Have you got that?"

Finch ambled over to the mirror in his motel room and examined the bruise and suture threads on his face. His left cheek ached and the ugly whorl of blacks, yellows and blues seemed to swim across his flesh. His index finger toyed with the engorged tissue at his earlobe. He frowned, then looked away and focused on the conversation. "Of course I get it. The problem is, I'm not going to get the credit. What if I write one of those first-person features you're so fond of?"

"Not yet. For the next week, this is news, not a feature. And you should know that," he added. His tone was on the verge of falling into a sophomore-level lecture. He decided to change tactics. "Anyway, you'll get full credit when you bring this out as a Pulitzer-winning book."

A book ... if only. Finch realized that with this fantasy, Wally was reaching deep to coax him along. He knew he'd have to capitulate sooner or later. Might as well be sooner. "All right, switch me over to Fiona when we're done. Then I'm coming home."

"Excellent. I'll get her to call you when she's free. She's on a breaking story over on Russian Hill. Meanwhile, is there anything I can get you from here?"

"Yeah. The name of a good dentist. I'm supposed to have some kind of follow-up next week. And make sure whoever you find is covered in the *eXpress's* medical package."

※

Finch packed his bag and checked out of the Prest Motel a little before noon. He still hadn't heard from Fiona and he knew he had one more visit to make before he drove over to Portland and began the long drive south along the I-5 to San Francisco.

Ten minutes later he pulled his car into the driveway at the Argyle's home. The shock on Millie Argyle's face when he stood at her front door reminded Finch of how horrible his injuries appeared. The emergency ward surgeon had assured him he'd be back to his "good-looking self within a week." But the doctor's advice faded whenever Finch encountered someone who didn't know about his beating and the subsequent shooting. Finch decided to keep a low profile in the coming weeks, but this visit to Ethan Argyle couldn't be avoided.

"Coffee?" Ethan pointed to a chair next to the dining table in the middle of the kitchen. "I brewed a fresh pot five minutes ago."

"Thanks, black." Finch sat and watched Argyle prepare the drinks. He set the cups on the table, no saucers, no spoons, no napkins, no spare chatter.

Argyle sat opposite Finch and studied his face a moment. "Looks like he got a piece of you."

"That he did," Finch said and steered his eyes away. He scanned the kitchen. The Argyles lived simply. A collection of family photos were fixed to the far wall, a calendar had been tacked next to the wall phone. A small collection of recipe books lay stacked under the cupboards, and a Sony ghetto-blaster sat on the counter, unplugged.

"Ethan, I think we both know you saved my life last night." The words seemed to ball together in his mouth. Finch tried to hold Argyle with his eyes, but Argyle looked away.

"You heard it was me, did you?" He turned his head to Finch and lowered his chin. "Someone told you that?"

"Yeah." Finch wondered if he should reveal his source. In this case, he realized it would be helpful. "Jennie Lee. She told me she was there during the shooting. She said that after the deputies disabled Gruman's truck, there was this pause, then he fired, hit my ear — and then you and the deputies let loose." He lifted a hand in the air and set it beside his coffee mug. "And ... that was the end."

"Did she tell you only one bullet hit Gruman?" His eyes narrowed and he took a sip of coffee.

Finch nodded. "And that you called it."

Argyle turned his head to one side but kept his eyes on Finch. He could trust him, he realized. These were simple facts being uttered. No accusations, no remorse.

"That's what shook me," he said. "Nine of us — and everyone else except me shot at the trees. I was the only one who lined him up and pulled the trigger. I just wasn't expecting that."

"I guess Gruman had them so full of fear, he figured no one would step up."

Argyle shrugged. "That's when I realized that things might go better, legally, if I acknowledged it right away. I knew the forensics tests would show the shot was mine anyway."

"I guess."

Argyle pulled himself up in his chair. He considered the facts which would never be confessed. What the sheriff had done to Millie when they were teenagers. And his own silent hatred of Gruman. At what point would they become *stated* facts, too? Never. Whatever else might emerge in a trial, he would keep them to himself and Millie and bury these truths along with Gruman's corpse.

"Look," Finch said, "I know you've got a long way to go before this clears up. But there's two people you can count on. One, Jennie Lee. Winslow brought her along as an independent observer so if things went south, she could be relied on to testify. And face it, she's credible. Two, me. I'll testify to exactly what happened. Explain I was in danger of losing my life. That you literally saved it." Now that he'd said this twice, he felt as if some basic restitution was in place. But he knew he could offer more.

"And Ethan, if there's anything I can do for you — and I mean *anything* — just say the word." He held his eyes and added, "I mean it."

Argyle nodded and thought a moment. "There might be," he said.

"Name it."

"In September Ben's probably heading down to Stanford. He's been offered a scholarship." He smiled, the first hint of optimism in his face that Finch had seen. "Anyway, we don't know a soul in that part of the state, and since it looks like I'll be tied up here, it'd be good to know that he could call someone. You know, if any trouble came up."

"Trouble? Forget *trouble,* I'll take him to lunch once a month just to make sure he's on track."

Argyle nodded. "That would help."

A moment of silence welled between them and Finch decided to continue. "You know, last night in the hospital I was thinking about Ben. About the trouble he got into with Donnel Smeardon. But that wasn't real trouble. That was nothing to worry about — it was just his *Michael Phelps Moment."* Finch emphasized these last three words as though they might indicate an historic achievement.

"His what?"

"Michael Phelps, the Olympic swimmer. Remember when he won his eighth gold medal at the 2008 Beijing Games? An honest-to-God world champion. Remember that? Then in

February 2009, the photo of him smoking ganja from a bong? That picture of him toking up was beamed all around the planet."

"Yeah. I remember that."

"Well, the time he spent with Donnel Smeardon was Ben's Michael Phelps Moment. He'd been so good for so long, he just needed to see what life was like on the other side. All the time he spent getting perfect grades, applying for scholarships, working on his Eagle scouts, shooting hoops in the gym — he could see the dark side over there, just out of his reach." Finch waved a hand to the back door, as if another reality lay at hand, even if it was beyond Ethan's imagination. "He simply needed to touch it, to see if it was real. Or just an illusion that would hold him back from living a full life."

Argyle rolled his eyes and laughed. "Sounds like you've been on the ganja a little too long, yourself."

"Not guilty. I gave the stuff up years ago." He laughed a genuine, heart-felt laugh that rose through his chest and provided a sense of release.

"Well, maybe you're right. Ben's a good boy. Always has been. I just mistook one thing he did — for something that he really didn't do at all." Argyle paused and his mood took a serious turn. He washed a hand over his face with a look of shame. "Sweet Mother of Mary, but doesn't this life make fools of us all."

"Almost once a day, in my case."

He turned his attention to Will and tried to recover their buoyant mood. "With talk like that," he said with a chuckle, "I think you need to get back to San Francisco. A fool's paradise

D. F. Bailey

if I ever saw one."

"Yeah, maybe so." Finch laughed once more, and for a
moment he felt the bond linking him with Ethan Argyle. It
carried a feeling of tenderness, without sentiment for the past
or any expectation that they would see one another again — a
moment of respect for all their differences and this strange
thread of death and escape from death that now tied their lives
together.

※

To maintain his invisibility on the drive back to San Francisco,
Finch decided to order all his meals from drive-through restau-
rants. As he approached the junction of the I-5 and 26 just west
of Portland, he stopped at a pull-out in Beaverton and ordered a
fruit smoothie. The dentist had advised him to eat only soft
foods for the next few days. Finch interpreted this to mean *eat
only food you can drink.* The idea depressed him, but as he
drove away from the take-out booth his phone rang and his
disposition brightened: Fiona's name flashed onto the screen.

"Wait a sec," he told her and parked ahead of the highway
on-ramp. A dozen cars whizzed past him. "Okay, I just had to
park."

"Where are you?" she asked. "Or more important, *how* are
you? Wally told me you've been shot and then hospitalized.
But as usual, no elaborate details from the man."

"I'm just coming into Portland." He glanced over his shoulder to read the sign of the restaurant behind him. To his surprise he could see a heavy fog bank rolling in from the west
coast, a bit of Astoria chasing him. "I'm parked next to
Wilma's Quik-Stop. And the details are that I was shot in the

earlobe, which is now missing in action, and then hospitalized for one night in the surprisingly efficient Columbia Memorial Hospital." He decided to omit news about his refurbished upper left molar and inserted a brief laugh to demonstrate that despite his wounds he could joke about it. "Oh yeah, and my face looks like Micky Mantle slugged me with a baseball bat. Or to be precise, a Smith & Wesson pistol. And do not start sobbing when you see me because I look much worse than I really am."

"Jesus, Will. That's terrible." She paused. "I literally don't know what to say."

"Seriously, no matter what it sounds like, I'm okay. I expect to be back at the *eXpress* this week."

"All right." She paused and her voice shifted to a lower, more serious tone. "Look, Wally assigned this job to me and I want you to know that I did *not* ask to do this story about you. Okay?"

"He told me." Finch watched an eighteen-wheeler whiz past him and head down the highway. Behind him he could see the first sheets of fog approaching his car. "And I get it. As of last night, I'm part of the story, therefore no longer reporting my role in it. And to be honest, of all the people in the *eXpress* who could write it, you are my first choice." Despite the pain in his cheek, he smiled.

Fiona took a moment to prepare for the interview and to clear her mind of the thoughts she'd had about Will. "All right, are you ready to go on record?"

"Let her rip."

"Okay, tell me in your own words what happened from the moment you arrived at Sheriff Mark Gruman's house. When you're done, I'll go back to ask you any unanswered questions."

A pro interviewing a pro. Finch knew she'd be recording this so he began the story as if he were writing it himself. That way he could ensure the story would be faithful to the facts, if not his perspective and style. He cleared his throat and began. "When a recorded conversation between Sheriff Mark Gruman and eighteen-year-old Donnel Smeardon, the recent victim of a premeditated murder, came into my hands, I decided to interview the sheriff to gather his response to the material on the recording...."

Finch spoke for about twenty minutes, time enough for him to relive the nightmare in detail. He shuddered when he considered what might have happened. When he finished, Fiona asked two more questions. First, did he have any idea when he drove to Gruman's house that he could be murdered himself? Second, how did the deaths of Smeardon and Gruman impact the new inquiry into Toeplitz's death?

Finch explained that while he thought Gruman might react negatively to the confrontation, he honestly didn't expect what happened. "Do you think I was reckless?" he asked her.

"Maybe." She paused and then continued, "I know I wouldn't have gone up there alone."

Finch's finger toyed with the stitches on his cheek as he pondered this. "Whatever," he said with a measure of self-doubt. After a moment he pressed on with his dictation.

"As for Toeplitz, things couldn't be more uncertain. Gruman died without ever confirming to me that he killed him, or Smeardon for that matter. I recorded the entire conversation, and there's not a hint of his confession. And he never confirmed that the Whitelaw twins were there. But I have testimony — and this is *off* the record, by the way — from Gianna, that tells their whole story. I just don't know where this thing can go from here. Which is crazy, because that's what brought me up here."

"Gianna? Okay, so hold that thought." Fiona paused as she wondered how to reveal her news. The fact that she'd held onto it for the past half-hour might make her seem manipulative. Maybe that would be the best approach: drop any possibility of manipulation and tell all. "Listen, I'm worried that you're going to think I've been holding back on you when you hear what I have to say."

"Hear what?"

"I *only* did it so I could get your interview straight before I filled you in."

Finch leaned forward and pressed a hand to his forehead. "Fiona, fill me in on what?"

Two more trucks pushed up the road, then disappeared through a curtain of mist.

"Gianna Whitelaw committed suicide last night."

"What?!" He felt himself gag.

"Believe me, it's true. Wally sent me over to her place on Russian Hill this morning to piece it together." She waited, a long pause. "She jumped from the Golden Gate Bridge. Her body was found below Pier 45 this morning. All the cable news stations are broadcasting the whole thing right now."

"I can't believe it," he moaned. Finch drew a hand over his eyes. He felt dizzy. Completely lost. "What a disaster."

"Yeah." She waited, as if the pause might restore his equanimity. "You need to get back here."

He thought about Gianna, about her soft, full body. Then about the insight he had lying in the hospital bed, his head ringing, earlobe shot off, jaw shut and swollen, his mind spinning with the impact of his own mortality and the deaths swirling around him. Toeplitz. Gruman. Smeardon. But most dear of all, Buddy — beautiful, lovely Buddy. Gone forever. That was his epiphany, the well-worn cliché, that only a life well-lived made death bearable.

"Are you all right?"

He drifted a moment and realized that everything had been destroyed. He had recordings of Gianna, Smeardon, and Gruman — all the sources who could verify the story. Now Gianna dead, too. He watched a little whorl of fog waltz across the sidewalk. A dog barked in the distance. Baying.

"Look, Fiona," he gasped. "Gianna didn't ... *kill herself.*" The words were supposed to sound convincing, but they fell from his tongue like wet spittle.

"Will, she posted a note. On Facebook." She paused. "Toeplitz was her lover, right?"

"I know. I know about her and Toeplitz. You don't have to tell me about that." He took a moment to gain control of his voice. "Fiona, just listen to me. *Gianna was murdered, too.*"

She said nothing. Better to let him rave than contradict his certainty.

He tried to think what to do. "I'm coming home," he said.

"Okay," she said. "Things will make more sense back here. I'm sure of it."

He clicked off his phone and stared into the gray fog that now surrounded him. A stream of cars and trucks crept through the bleak shroud, crawling toward him from both directions and then vanishing into the mist as they slipped away. He flicked on the headlights, set his fingers on the car keys and wondered when he would find the strength to start the ignition.

Soon, he whispered to himself, soon. Then he would make his way home. And find Gianna's killer.

READ THE COMPLETE WILL FINCH TRILOGY

Bone Maker — A death in the wilderness. A woman mourns alone. A reporter works a single lead. Can Will Finch break the story of murder and massive financial fraud? Or will he become the Bone Maker's next victim?

Stone Eater — A reporter on the rebound. An ex-cop with nothing to lose. A murder they can only solve together. Sparks fly when Will Finch agrees to work with Eve Noon to uncover a murder plot. But can they unmask the Stone Eater before he destroys them both?

Lone Hunter — One billion dollars. Two killers. Three ways to die. Will Finch and Eve Noon bait the trap. But could their clever ploy trigger catastrophe when two killers battle for a billion dollar prize? Or can Will and Eve defeat their most cunning adversary yet?

ENJOY THESE OTHER NOVELS BY D. F. BAILEY

Fire Eyes — a W.H. Smith First Novel Award finalist
"Fire Eyes is a taut psychological thriller with literary overtones, a very contemporary terrorist romance."
— Globe and Mail

Healing the Dead
"You start reading Healing the Dead with a gasp and never get a proper chance to exhale."
— Globe and Mail

The Good Lie
"A tale that looks at a universal theme...that readers are going to love."
— Boulevard Magazine

Exit from America
"Another great story of moral revelation, despair and redemption by a contemporary master."
— Lawrence Russell, culturecourt.com

Made in the USA
Las Vegas, NV
23 July 2022

52053822R00142